MW01633325

RESCUING HI`ILANI (SPECIAL FORCES: OPERATON ALPHA)

DELTA FORCE HAWAII

REINA TORRES

This book is a work of fiction. Names, characters, places, and incidents are products of the author's imagination or used fictitiously. Any resemblance to actual events or locales or persons living or dead is entirely coincidental.

© 2018 ACES PRESS, LLC. ALL RIGHTS RESERVED

No part of this work may be used, stored, reproduced or transmitted without written permission from the publisher except for brief quotations for review purposes as permitted by law.
This book is licensed for your personal enjoyment only. This book may not be re-sold or given away to other people. If you would like to share this book with another person, please purchase an additional copy for each recipient. If you're reading this book and did not purchase it, or it was not purchased for your use only, please purchase your own copy.

Dear Readers,

Welcome to the Special Forces: Operation Alpha Fan-Fiction world!

If you are new to this amazing world, in a nutshell the author wrote a story using one or more of my characters in it. Sometimes that character has a major role in the story, and other times they are only mentioned briefly. This is perfectly legal and allowable because they are going through Aces Press to publish the story.

This book is entirely the work of the author who wrote it. While I might have assisted with brainstorming and other ideas about which of my characters to use, I didn't have any part in the process or writing or editing the story.

I'm proud and excited that so many authors loved my characters enough that they wanted to write them into their own story. Thank you for supporting them, and me!

READ ON!
Xoxo
Susan Stoker

CHAPTER 1

When Jackson Guard reached his Commander's front door he knocked at the heavy wooden surface with a short, succinct rap of his knuckles. He stepped back and waited for an answer and got it faster than he expected. Peering around the corner, the commander waved him closer. "I'm on the lanai in the back. Come around."

Picking his way along the flagstone pathway, he smelled the pungent scent of the *lau`ae* ferns along the way. It was a scent that he'd never experienced before moving to Hawaii, and it had quickly become a scent he'd never forget. It was clean and cool, if cool could have a scent, and it relaxed him in an odd way.

Turning at the corner of the house he caught sight of the broad lanai tucked into the side of the house, the rattan furniture all but empty except for his commander. Two oddly colored dogs ran around the yard playing a game of keep away with a rag-doll toy, barely taking notice of the newcomer in their midst.

"Come and have a seat, Ajax."

Gesturing to the empty chair beside him, he leaned back and lifted a leg, setting his ankle on his knee.

The commander's oddly casual appearance put a strange knot in Jackson's middle. He took the seat beside his superior officer, but he didn't sink back into the seat, instead perching on the edge of the seat.

Almost as if he'd hit a switch, the two dogs rushed at him, the one on the right dropped the slobbery toy at the tip of his boot. The two dogs as one nodded at the toy and then looked up at him expectantly. When he didn't move instantly, they did it again.

Commander Chastain chuckled. "They've adopted you."

"You mean they've decided to make me their servant?"

The commander nodded. "Basically."

Leaning forward, Jackson picked up the toy by his fingertips hoping to keep most of the slobber off of him, failing miserably.

He flung it off into the far corner of the yard behind what looked like a tangled hedge of colorful croton plants and the dogs took off like a shot almost taking them both down in a tangle of legs and yips.

"I asked you to come over to ask a favor of you."

Turning to look at his commander, he nodded, slipping back into the role of subordinate in a heartbeat. "Yes, sir."

Picking up a glass of iced tea, the commander gestured at the glass beside Jackson on the table. Jackson shook his head.

"No, thank you, sir."

"With the rest of your unit taking advantage of their leave I have to impose upon you to do something."

Jackson nodded.

"We have two Delta Force members visiting Hawaii from Texas. I would like for you to meet with them and let them know what might be of interest for them to see and experience while they're here in the Islands."

"You want me to play tour guide?"

His commander gave him a measuring look. "I'm not expecting you to take them all over the island wearing an Aloha Shirt and a kukui nut lei.

"Meet with them for a meal, point out the interesting places you and your teammates have visited. It's just a nice thing to do." He took another sip of his drink and set down his glass as the dogs chased each other in and out of the bushes. One whistle and the two dogs disentangled themselves and rushed at him like he was holding all the food hostage. Once he'd given each dog a liberal head and belly scratch he looked up at Jackson.

"What do you say, Ajax? Do me a favor?"

Jackson drew in a breath and let it out in one slow motion. "I don't see how I can refuse, but I'll do it because they're our brothers just as much as my own men are. I'm just not the kind of guy who does real well playing tour guide."

Commander Chastain's smile rode the line between smug and a long-suffering silence. "I'm not asking you to give them a kidney or a lung."

Jackson gave him a knowing nod. "That would be easier."

The Commander sat back in his chair and gestured to

the corner of the house. "Why don't you just go before I order the dogs to lick you into submission."

Jackson stood up and gave his commanding officer a well-practiced salute and left, pulling out his phone when it beeped in his back pocket. By the time he got to the curb he was shaking his head.

The text message was from the Commander with the names of the two Deltas and their room numbers at the Hale Koa hotel.

"Well, this should be fun."

❧

And surprisingly, it was.

He'd met up with Truck and Ghost in Waikiki at the Hale Koa Hotel's poolside bar the next morning, for the better part of an hour they chatted about the islands and what the Deltas already had planned, offering up ideas of what else they might want to do or see while they were on island for the next week.

Maybe it was the fact that he lived in Hawaii but there was something about these men that he admired on sight. They were… happy. At ease.

They seemed to just enjoy being in the moment.

Something that Jackson hadn't managed to do in over a year. Not since he broke up with-

"Hey," Ghost sat forward on his chair and slid a glance to Truck sitting beside him, "I hope you don't mind, but we're expecting to be interrupted in a minute or two."

"Interrupted?" Instantly alert, Jackson sat up. "I'm here if you need back-up."

Truck's smile confused him. "Don't worry, we can handle these two with our eyes closed."

Ghost gave his friend a look of concern. "Oh, we can, can we? Did you hit your head on your way down here?"

There was too much playful banter in their words for this to be anything dangerous, but still, it was more than a little confusing for Jackson.

He wouldn't trade his team for any other in the whole world. They'd been working together for the last year, some of them had met before that, or had missions together in other capacities, but there was a surety of trust that Jackson felt when his team was near.

Before they'd left, there had been a good helping of humor, teasing each other about being lonely. Jackson had laughed it off, but seeing how these two were together, he did have to admit that he did miss his compatriots.

Not that he'd tell them.

He'd never hear the end of it.

No, the last thing he'd ever tell the guys is that he missed them.

Jackson almost shuddered at the thought.

But even as much as he enjoyed working with his men and how close they were, they were all focused on one thing when they were together. The mission.

Even if they didn't have one they were actively involved in, they were always looking ahead.

There was always some situation on the horizon and they were constantly working to keep themselves ready to go in a heartbeat.

On edge.

Like a racecar at the line, the driver waiting for the lights to change.

Perched on the edge of the cliff, ready to base jump and plummet toward the ground.

But not these men.

There was something different about these two Deltas that went down to the core.

"Hey there!"

Jackson turned and looked at the two women who were approaching the table and watched as they sauntered up in sundresses and shades, their heads uncovered.

The men across from him watched the ladies with interest and sat back in their chairs, smiling.

"We just had the most amazing time at the spa." The first woman to the table was tall and slender, her hair colored in a gradated rush of color that looked like pink and red flames. If he had to guess, it had been brown at one time, but with the fresh dye job she'd probably applied the color before coming to Hawaii. "I don't suppose you gentlemen would mind sharing the table with us?"

Jackson looked across at the men but found no sign that either one would refuse.

In fact, he saw more than a few signs that the men would welcome the interruption.

Oh, right.

The other woman, a brunette with color so natural it had to be, or she had an amazing stylist. She leaned into her friend, but her eyes were on the men.

Correction, her eyes were on Ghost.

"If not, we could always go to the pool and see if we

could find a couple of the pool boys who might be willing to put sunscreen on our backs for us."

Ghost didn't hesitate. One moment he was sitting back in his chair and then next, he had the woman on his lap, wrapped in his arms.

He pressed a kiss to her cheek and then grumbled into her ear. "If you need sunscreen, I'm going to be the one putting it on you."

The other woman was moving before he noticed that Truck was starting to get out of his chair.

The woman with fire-like hair pushed her hand on his shoulder and he sat back dutifully as she rounded the chairs and flopped down onto his lap.

Jackson had no doubt that if Truck hadn't wanted to sit, he could have shrugged off the woman's touch.

And when he saw how she tried to wrap her hands around his wrists and lift them up, Truck eagerly helping her with the task, ended up with his arms around the woman, his head turning to press a kiss to her neck.

Ghost spoke, turning his attention back. "This is the interruption we were telling you about." He rushed on when the woman in his lap opened her mouth, obviously ready to take him to task for his comment. "Calm down, sweetheart. It was a joke." Shaking his head with a good-natured smile on his lips, Ghost explained further. "Jackson, these two amazing women are our wives. Rayne is my wife, finally," he winced when Rayne pushed an elbow back into his middle, "and the woman who conquered Truck, that's Mary. Don't get them mad, ever. They know how to take men like us apart."

Mary and Rayne nodded, but it was Mary that spoke.

"And feed them to the sharks. So don't get any ideas, gentlemen."

Listening to the banter between the couples, how they interacted with each other, Jackson knew he was in over his head.

Wives.

Holy sh-

"You okay, Jackson?"

It took him a minute to remember the name of Truck's wife. "I'm fine, Mary, thanks. It's just a bit of a shock."

"Shock?" She gave him a shrewd once over. "Why?"

Before he could answer, Truck reached over and took Mary's hand, lifting it up to his lips for a kiss. A quick look over at Ghost and Rayne and Jackson saw a flash of intimate laughter between the two.

"You look like you've been hit by a two-by-four, Ajax."

He turned and met Truck's eyes and saw the humor in his expression. The other Delta Force member wasn't making fun of him, or maybe he was, but it was all in good fun. There was no malice in the gesture. They were compatriots and they were brothers even though they hadn't met before that day.

"Not so much a two-by-four," Mary gave him a sly look, "I think we've messed with his head on the inside."

Rayne wasn't going to be left out. "If you're worried about PDA, we'll try to keep it to a minimum."

Mary shook her head. "Sorry, I'm in paradise with my man... PDA is going to happen."

Truck touched a quick kiss to the top of his wife's head. "You know it."

Jackson held up his hands in surrender. "I have

nothing against your PDA. It's just that we've always been told that Delta Force is a lonely road. Commander Chastain has been adamant in his rationale. So, seeing the four of you, obviously happy-"

"Ridiculously happy," Rayne interjected before Ghost brushed a kiss along her cheek.

Mary stepped in next, leaning forward to talk. "So everyone in your unit is single?"

Jackson nodded.

"No one has a girlfriend?"

It didn't take more than a moment for him to squirm under her close scrutiny. "No."

Rayne met Mary's eyes for a second. If he hadn't been looking at Mary, he would have missed the gesture. As a pair, the women turned to look at him.

"Why not?"

Ghost sat up, wrapped his arm around his wife's waist, and leaned into her side. "Are you actually interrogating him?"

Mary jumped to her friend's defense. "Absolutely." She leaned further forward on the table and Jackson saw Truck reach down and grab a hold of the back of her pants. Jackson wasn't sure if he was securing his wife from slipping off the edge of her seat or climbing over the table to shake him, but either way, he found himself smiling ear to ear.

"There's no use for an interrogation, it's just the way we do things. The Commander says no relationships and we follow his order."

"Order?" Now Rayne sounded incensed. She looked at her husband with a narrowed glare. "Can they do that?"

Ghost lifted his hand and brushed some stray hairs back behind her ear. "It's a fine line," he agreed, "but back when we met, I think all of us felt the same way. Our responsibilities and duties made it difficult to think of bringing a relationship into the equation."

"Equation?" Rayne gave him a little smirk. "Applying math and science to love? That's either going to get you smacked or…"

Jackson turned away when Ghost pulled his wife in for a kiss. One look at Truck and Mary told him this wasn't an unusual occurrence for their friends.

But that also left Truck to pick up the string of their conversation. "And some of us tried to fight it, but over time every single guy in our unit realized they didn't stand a chance trying to ignore the simple fact that we'd all found the woman that was 'the' woman. After that, it was all we could do to beg, plead, and grovel hoping that they'd take pity on us."

Mary elbowed her husband and Jackson saw the much larger man over-dramatize his wince of pain for comic effect. It certainly put a smile on his wife's face. "It took a lot of begging from both of them but Rayne and I made honest men out of them."

Jackson felt his face blanch and it was Truck who came to his rescue when he set his hands on Mary's waist and pulled her up off of the ground and slanted a big kiss over her lips. When he was done, he leaned back but he didn't set her back down on the ground.

His wife gave him a good-natured shove and laughed out loud when he finally put her down.

The noise tightened in Jackson's gut. He'd heard

laughter like that before. He'd had a woman wrap her arms around his neck like Mary did, and he'd had a woman lean into his kiss like-

Clearing his throat, he looked at the four. "What are you doing for the rest of the day?"

Ghost spoke for them. "Nothing really. We were going to have breakfast with you and then see where it goes from there."

"I was wondering if you wanted to see a concert tonight."

It was Ghost who answered first. "What concert?"

Letting out a long pent-up breath he looked at the ladies first and then the guys. "It's more of a showcase. Hawaiian music and dance at the Old Hawaii Theater. It's this Art-Deco theater downtown that you'll never forget once you see it."

Mary and Rayne shared a look before Rayne looked back at him. "You're a Hawaiian music fan?"

That's when he felt a muscle in his jaw tick and both of the ladies perked up. He knew he was treading a dangerous line. "I've been introduced to some great music since I've been here. We have one Country Music station and that one," he grimaced, "the DJs are jerks and the music repetitious. But since you're in Hawaii you should at least hear some of the music and see some dancing that might be a little more authentic than some of the shows here in Waikiki." He let the subject drop and waited for the four to think it over.

Oddly enough, it wasn't the women that spoke up. Truck, leaned down and looked him square in the face, searching his eyes. "Who is she?"

Jackson pulled back a little and gave him what he hoped was a confused expression. "What are you talking about?"

Truck laughed. "Son, you got it bad for someone. I'm gonna guess that she's either going to see the show or…" He let his words trail off but his eyes continued to bore through Jackson's skull.

"Okay, so I know one of the performers. She's singing and dancing in the show, but I'm not just inviting you because I want to see her, it's a good show and I think you'll enjoy it-"

"We'd love to go." Mary smacked Truck on the arm and while he winced and grimaced at his wife, she rolled her eyes. "I think our men could use a little culture."

Ghost gave his wife a smile. "We're here to see the sights and enjoy ourselves. Why not?"

Jackson turned a thankful look at the ladies. "I don't suppose you ladies wanted to wear something with a local flair?"

Rayne and Mary shared conspiratory grins before they turned back to Jackson and nodded. "Yes!"

Pulling his phone from his pocket he opened the contacts and scrolled through to the T's. When the call was picked up, he heard the soft spoken words of the store's owner. "Auntie Lina? This is Jackson Guard, yes… yes… it's been too long, sorry." He listened as she prattled on for a moment and he saw the curious looks from the ladies. When she finally came up for breath, Jackson threw himself into the breech like a man ready to protect his team by throwing himself down on a bomb. "Great…

that's great, Auntie. I'll have the ladies come by the store. My treat."

Mary leaned back against Truck. "I'm going to like it here in Hawaii."

§

The grassy expanse in the center of the Royal Shopping Center in Waikiki was a picturesque spot. It better be, considering the year of construction and the amount of money they spent on landscaping the little 'park' at the center of it.

On any given day you could go down, grab a cup of coffee at the adjacent coffee shop and sit under the banyan tree and enjoy the tropical weather. And then, depending on the time of day there could be live music, native crafts, or dance performances and lessons.

Hi`ilani Ahfong was one of their well-loved performers in both music and dance, but some of her favorite moments at the mall were the days she got to teach dance.

Seven little girls and one adorable little boy had been learning a song that was popular among the children of Hawaii. Not only did they love learning the name of the raucous bird that no one could seem to ignore, but they sang with gusto!

"Sassy little mynah bird, with your funny walk," the little girls in the front row were doing an admirable job of remembering the steps, but there were two girls in the back row struggling a bit, so she moved through the front line and stepped in front of the two, doing the dance backwards so they could follow.

"My you are a noisy bird…"

"Over here, girls!" She heard a bunch of old-fashioned camera clicks and saw a few telling flashes of light. "Smile so I can show your grandma how much fun we're having!"

One of the girls looked up with a wince on her face and the other beamed from ear to ear.

Hi`ilani moved on down the line and gently turned one of the girls in the opposite direction so she could fall in line with the other children. Looking up with a grin missing her front teeth, the bouncy blonde gushed out a thank you. "This is just like line dancing with different music!"

"Glad you're enjoying it," she nudged the girl in the other direction so she'd be back in line with the others. "Don't forget the ending."

Stepping around the group and off to the side she crouched down and placed her index finger in front of her mouth when the song ended so that the children remembered the last motion telling the bird to be quiet and everyone sang. "*Kuli kuli e!*"

A rousing cheer rose up from the curious onlookers and scores of cameras flashed around the eight children. Moments later, Hi`ilani was inundated with requests for pictures and even some autographs. It was a heady rush of movement and smiles, certainly more exhausting than teaching or dancing. Both of those activities were as natural to her as breathing.

Dealing with the public and fans could be fun, but for the last year she'd been struggling to keep that happy face on when it was a matter of these moments. It only served to remind her that there was a hole in her life.

A life that had been so much better. Better when she was with Jackson Guard.

"Hey there, girlie!"

Hi`ilani shook herself from her reverie. She knew that larger than life booming voice and the crazy energetic woman that it came from. CeeCee Fordham was an agent who had blown into her life a few months before.

After performing at a private party at an estate near Diamond Head, CeeCee had approached her about representation, determined to steal her away from whoever was representing her, only to discover that Hi`ilani didn't have an agent. Yet.

Turning to greet CeeCee, she saw the sparkle in the older woman's eyes. "What's going on?"

"Are you sitting down?"

Hi`ilani looked down and then back at her agent. They were both obviously standing, facing each other, but inconsequential things like that didn't bother CeeCee apparently.

"Because I have some news for you!"

"Ooohkay," she waited for her to say something. "What's the news?"

"Remember that audition I sent you on?"

"You mean one of the dozen you've sent me to in the last two months?" She shrugged. "I remember, but I don't know which one you're talking about."

When her agent's eyes widened, Hi`ilani took in a short gasping breath.

"What happened, CeeCee? Tell me!"

"I just got a call back from Jim Hutchins."

Hi`ilani's mind was working double time trying to match the name to a memory, but it wasn't working.

"Jim Hutchins saw your audition tape and given the notes he got from the casting director, he's going to cast you in Honolulu P.I."

The words made it into her ears. She understood them at some level.

But it wasn't until she realized that the reason she couldn't breathe was that her agent was trying to suffocate her in a hug that the enormity of that moment really sunk in.

She was going to be on a Network Drama Television show.

"I'm going to be on TV." The words sounded heavy and dull in her voice. "I think I need to sit down."

"See?" CeeCee laughed loud enough to scare away a few pigeons that had been milling around their feet. "I told you to sit down!"

Releasing Hi`ilani from her hug, CeeCee wrapped her arm around her protégé's shoulders and started to walk her toward the locker room to get her things.

"Look, I'll take you out to celebrate and then we'll make plans. We'll have to get you a lawyer to look over the contract and then we'll get totally drunk at Hula's bar and hang with the guys for fun."

Hi`ilani stopped short and looked up at her agent. "I can't. Not tonight." She nervously licked at her lips. "I have that showcase tonight at the Old Hawaii Theater. Maybe we can meet tomorrow? I need some time to process this moment."

"You're not thinking of passing on this, right?" CeeCee almost sounded panicked.

"No way!" Hi`ilani smiled up at her and gave her a big hug before stepping back. "It's just out of left field. I didn't think I had a chance at all of getting the part. It still doesn't feel real."

CeeCee nodded. "That's the difference between you and me, girlie! I knew from the moment I saw you performing that you were destined for big things… HUGE things! And I'm not just talking about men." CeeCee gave her a wink and raised her brows in a comical expression.

"I'm not talking about men at all," Hi`ilani sighed.

"Well, that's going to change too," CeeCee assured her. "This is just the beginning of the exciting life you're going to have!"

They paused outside of the locker room door and CeeCee narrowed her eyes at her.

"Are you okay, sweetie?"

Hi`ilani blinked back the tears that pricked at the backs of her eyes. Since the moment she'd heard the good news from CeeCee, everything inside of her told her to call two phone numbers. The first, her family. She wanted to tell her dad, her tutu, and her sisters. And then she wanted to call Jackson. It was crazy, right?

He'd dumped her a little over a year ago. Told her he didn't have a place for her in his life. And seriously, she'd dated after him.

Okay one guy.

And that, well that ended because try as she did to like Kyle. He just wasn't Jackson.

She sighed and hung her head. She was crazy with maybe just a hint of pathetic mixed in, but it didn't change the fact that she missed him like air.

But that was her problem.

Try as she might she hadn't been able to shake him out of her life. And so here she was-

"Wow, even I can hear the gears turning in your head. Look, go, get changed. I'll drop you off at the theater so you don't have to take *theBus*. You know that traffic can be killer at this hour."

Hi`ilani rose up on her toes to kiss CeeCee on the cheek. "Thanks, CeeCee. *Mahalo* for everything you've done for me."

"Girlie, you're worth it."

CHAPTER 2

Jackson watched the cab pull up to the curb in front of the theater and then jogged out to open the back-passenger door. Offering a hand to Rayne, he helped her out and then did the same for Mary. The two women looked resplendent in their brand new *mu`umu`u* from Auntie Lina's shop.

He couldn't help the appreciative looks he gave the women. Rayne's dress was a classic gown with loose belled sleeves that ended up above her elbows, moving graceful around her shoulders and Mary's dress had a velvet faced neckline and slim sleeves that accentuated her form. Both women's gowns were made from fabric with dark jeweled tones and simple floral patterns in silhouette. There was just something incredibly attractive about happy people and Mary and Rayne were obviously happy. It wasn't just because they were on vacation, just one look at either woman, or either couple for that matter, it was easy to tell they were all crazy happy and in love.

Someone clapped a hand down on his shoulder… hard.

"You might want to direct your eyes elsewhere, Ajax."

He would have laughed if Truck's hand on his shoulder wasn't bordering on agony. "They both look amazing," pain lanced through his shoulder – how the man managed to pinch a nerve with an open hand, Jackson would never know, "I wasn't trying to be disrespectful."

"And he wasn't," Rayne gave Truck a pointed look. "Besides, it's nice to know people appreciate the way we look. Let him go."

His arms started to go numb as Mary stepped closer. Jackson felt the hem of her dress brushing against the leg of his dress pants. She gave Truck a poke right in the center of his chest. "He's being nice. Stop before you do permanent damage."

A moment later he had feeling back down to his fingertips, but it was like pins and needles. He contemplated asking Truck to put his hand back on his shoulder before it became unbearable and then changed his mind when Mary touched her hand to his chest.

She looked over his dress uniform and gave him a look of appreciation. "Lookin' good, Ajax."

"Come 'ere, woman." Truck had her tucked up against his side in a heartbeat. "Don't make me take the boy apart."

Jackson wisely kept silent and still even after the 'boy' comment. He wasn't 'that' stupid.

"I was just telling him he looks good."

"I agree," Rayne earned herself a kiss brushed against her cheek and a murmured comment from her husband that made her laugh. "You stop, too. He's trying to make a good impression tonight. He doesn't need you two scaring him before he sees her."

Truck grunted and looked him over from head to toe. "He looks like he's got a stick up his butt."

Mary slugged him on the shoulder and Truck made a good show of rubbing the spot with a wince.

"Careful," he warned her, "you break me, you've bought me."

Moving his hand away, Mary rubbed at his arm. "Don't worry, big guy. If I break you, I'll put you right back together."

The expression on Truck's face changed in a heartbeat and suddenly he saw the truth of why the other Delta unit worked 'with spouses.' Mary and Rayne, they didn't take anything away from the soldier they were with. Even if Mary could bring out such a tender emotion in her husband, their love strengthened him. Made him a better soldier as well as a better man because she was there for him and he, for her.

The more he thought about it, he knew he was doing the right thing. He'd cross the line with Commander Chastain when he'd made things right with Hi`ilani.

She deserved that or he didn't deserve her.

Ghost gave him an appraising look and nodded. "Pulling out the fancy uniform?"

Jackson nodded. "It's only fair. I told her I couldn't be with her because of the Army. If I'm going to beg her forgiveness, she should get it from all of me, the soldier and the man."

"Aww." Mary leaned against Truck, wrapping her hands around his arm. "That's just too sweet."

"Come on, man." Truck shook his head. "You're trying to show us up."

"Not me," Jackson coughed out a laugh, "I'm trying to learn from your example. You've got your lives together. I've got to step up my game. If she tells me I don't have a chance…"

"You can't think of it like that." Mary's voice may have been soft in the din of the gathering crowd, but it reached his heart better than it reached his ears. "Truck didn't give up on me. I'm afraid to say he could have given up on me a bunch of times and I wouldn't have blamed him."

"Never, babe." The big man set a hand on her shoulder and leaned down to place a kiss on the top of her head. "I always knew you were mine."

Jackson felt his heart pound against his ribs as if it was trying to break free of its cage. "I'm glad you're all here tonight. I feel like I have my team at my back."

"We're here for you, Ajax." Ghost's eyes met his and Jackson felt the truth of his words. They had his back.

A kind of energy rolled through the crowd as they saw some ushers moving through the theater lobby and Jackson stepped to the side so Mary could see in through the glass doors.

Mary touched Jackson's arm. "This is kind of exciting for me." He turned to listen as the crowd shifted near the doors, eager to get in. "I was hoping to see some dancing and hear some Hawaiian music, but I didn't want to bore Truck."

Suddenly the space beside him was empty and he heard Mary's breathy squeal as Truck pulled her into his large body. He half-nuzzled her cheek as he growled into her ear. "Nothing you want to do would bore me, woman. Whatever makes you happy, makes me happy."

Jackson felt his stomach twist and drop like it had climbed into a roller coaster. Those words, that feeling. It was all so familiar and yet it felt like it was lightyears away.

"You okay, Ajax?"

Shaking himself free of his reverie he looked at Rayne and mustered up a smile. "Sure. Thanks for asking. It's still a little disconcerting," he confessed. "I've been thinking about her for the last year and it's felt like I was mourning the loss of half of me. I'd just kept telling myself that it was for the best. For her. For me," he swallowed hard, "it's been hell."

He looked down at the bouquet tucked under his arm and blew out a breath. "If I'm lucky, she won't throw this in my face."

Rayne smiled at him as she set a comforting hand on his shoulder. "If you'd like us to talk to her, Mary and I would be happy to."

Ghost brushed a kiss on his wife's cheek. "I love that you're so positive about this, but she might not be so eager to jump back in so quickly when he tells her that he's Delta before our vacation is over."

"Positive thoughts, please." Rayne's smile dipped a little at the corners, but Mary picked up the thought.

"Then they can come and visit us in Texas. She can meet all the women."

Ghost groaned softly and looked at Ajax. "Make sure you're in for good before introducing her to all of our women. If she's at all on the fence, she may go running and - ow!"

"What the hell, woman?"

Ghost leaned to the side as more ushers appeared in the lobby. Some continued up the stairs on either side of the lobby and the rest formed two long lines in preparation.

"That was just a taste of what you'll get if word gets back to the others about what you said."

He used his hands to intercept hers as she tried to pinch him again. "It was a joke!"

Rayne's eyes narrowed at him. "It better be."

A side door opened and a tiny woman stepped out, dressed in a floral print gown with a high-collar ending just under her chin. Her elegant hairstyle was made even more classic by the silver hairs tracing through her darker strands.

Ajax murmured his apologies and stepped off to the side to speak with her.

"Aunty Skinny. You might not remember me, but-"

"Oh, I remember you, Army man." Her voice was soft but the edge in it was telling. "You better not be here to cause trouble."

He shook his head, adamant in his tone. "I want to apologize to her when she'll let me," he explained, "but first, I was wondering if you could send these flowers back to her dressing room."

She gave him another look and then flickered a glance over at the two couples. "Those the ones that went into the shop today?"

He nodded. He thought that Lina would tell her sister and he'd been right. "The ladies are on vacation and wanted something beautiful to wear."

She gave him the slightest smile. "You trying to make nice?"

"I'm trying to make up to Hi`ilani for what I did. But I didn't send them to your shop just to be nice, they love their dresses."

She gave him a smile full of pride. "Good. I'll take her the flowers, but you hurt her again, *I going kick you somewhere gonna drop you to your knees, hmm?*"

He could tell from the look in her eyes that she meant it. "Never again, Auntie. Never again."

She narrowed her eyes at him and stared as if she could see right through him straight to his heart.

"*K'den.*" She held out her hand and he gave her the bouquet.

Then she turned her cheek toward him.

Laughing, he leaned forward and pressed a kiss on her cheek. "Thanks, Auntie."

She glared at him, telling him with a look that he should know better.

"*Mahalo*, Auntie."

Smiling with joy, she gave him an approving nod. "*A`ole pilikia.*"

She disappeared into the lobby leaving him to return to the others.

Mary was the first to pipe up. "Looks like you passed the first hurdle. So she's Hi`ilani's aunt?"

"No." He continued on because he knew how the conversation was going to go since he'd gone through it himself. "Here you can use Auntie or Uncle for someone close to you… someone at least a little older than you. But careful, if you use it with someone you don't know they might think you're calling them old."

The group laughed and all four of them swore to avoid that particular situation, Truck finishing it off for all of them. "I didn't come to Hawaii to get into a fight."

The main doors to the lobby opened up and the crowd started to move forward. Jackson let the ladies and their husband's go first while he took a steadying breath.

Ghost must have seen him go still. He turned around and looked at him. "No second guessing it now. Let's go."

ॐ

Hi`ilani looked into the mirror and tried to reconcile the woman before her with the woman she was inside, excited and brimming with possibilities. The face looking back at her was a little melancholy, a little down, and no amount of make-up would fix it.

She looked at her phone on the top of the counter and bit into her bottom lip. She still had Jackson's phone in her contacts. Sure, she'd removed it from her speed dial, but that really didn't matter. Hi`ilani didn't even need it saved in her phone.

His phone number was stored in her memory.

Going nowhere. Just like her thoughts.

Jackson had brought a new kind of joy into her world. He'd swept her off her feet and while it hadn't been like that scene in 'An Officer And A Gentleman,' but the feeling had been the same.

Life with him in it had been a rush of all kinds of emotions as well as all the amazing physical things that went with it, but right before she'd decided to tell him that she was in love with him, he broke up with her.

His life was too dangerous. He wanted to protect her.

She dropped her blush brush down onto the counter top and let out a loud groaning sigh.

"Uh oh," a voice reached her from the door, "sounds like you might need these."

Hi`ilani turned in her seat and stared. Auntie Skinny, one of her most favorite *calabash* family members. "Aloha, Auntie." Hi`ilani started to stand and greet her, but Auntie waved her back into her chair.

"I have to get back out to the house and help people find their seats, but someone wanted me to bring this to you." Walking closer, she held out the large bouquet of flowers. "Here. Take them."

The flowers were a mix of flowers in half a dozen colors. Roses, dendrobiums, tuberose, and a few others that Hi`ilani couldn't name off hand with her brain turning to mush. She didn't have to open the card inside the armful of flowers. The handwriting was all too familiar to her.

"Jackson."

"He's in the audience tonight with some friends." Auntie grinned. "I told him not to be stupid, or I'd *karang his alas.*"

Hi`ilani felt her cheeks warm at the idea that her teeny tiny Auntie Skinny would threaten Jackson with bodily harm… especially 'that' part of his body. Still… "How scared was he?"

"Enough," she sounded proud of herself. "You think he's here to apologize? Ask you out?"

Like a pail of cold water splashing over her, Hi`ilani sighed. "I don't know, but that's going to have to wait until after the show anyway."

Hi`ilani lifted the bouquet and drank in the scent of it, brushing her cheek against the silken petals before setting it down on the counter.

"I've got a job to do."

"You have an audience to dazzle." Auntie Skinny's smile lifted her spirits. "And an Army man in dress uniform watching your every mood."

"Auntie," Hi`ilani sighed, "you're not helping."

The older woman gave her an arch look. "I can tell by the look on his face, you don't need my help. Give him a chance, Hi`i. I know you've missed him."

"Well," she hedged, "I'll talk to him later. Okay?"

Auntie shrugged and turned away, letting her voice trail after her. "He looks damn good in that uniform. So *ono*."

Now her cheeks had to be fire red with the heat she felt. Having her auntie saying that Jackson looked delicious? She had to get herself together before she went on stage and forgot her lyrics or chords.

Less than a half an hour later, she was in the wings trying to sneak a look through the grate behind the ornamental molding. She had to be careful. The old adage was true in theater – if you could see them, they can see you.

So there she was trying to see through the minute spaces between the slats of wood that hid the backstage from the audience and still trying to see where Jackson was sitting.

"What's up with you, sis?"

She shook her head. She didn't have to look to know who was standing behind her. Kaleo Hubbard was a rising star in the music world. Just like his father and uncle, he had a rich voice that paired perfectly with both the older style of Hawaiian music and some of the newer sounds that were building a younger audience. They'd been friends forever.

"Nothing. Just waiting for Mackie to introduce me."

"Right," she heard his burst of laughter, "who are you looking for?"

She struggled to keep her voice even. "Jackson's in the audience."

"Ha! I knew it. *Haole* boy walks out on you and here you are-"

"Don't start, Kaleo."

"Did you invite him?" He stepped up beside her and squinted through the slats even with his eyes. He was a good half-foot taller than she was.

She shook her head. "I haven't talked to him since… you know."

Kaleo mimed crying his eyes out as he stood beside

her which only ended up within him getting a pinch in his side.

"Hey!"

"*Kuli kuli,*" she told him and he stuck his tongue out at her since she was trying to shush him like a child.

His mood changed quickly. He narrowed his gaze at her. "You goin' take him back?"

She heard the hard edge in his tone. All joking aside, he'd been her friend since *small kid days,* and he'd seen how much she suffered when Jackson had broken things off with her. "I haven't talked to him. Not even sure I want to do that."

"*Mo' bettah* you leave him alone, Sis. If he hurts you again, *I going drop kick him into the Ala Wai and let him sink.*"

"I'm not sure if I should hug you or hit you," she was laughing softly.

He shrugged. "*Whatevah you like. Jus' don't let him jerk you around, 'eh?*"

"Yes, sir." She saw the tight pinch of his lips at her playful answer. "I promise, okay?"

He saw Uncle Mackie heading for the microphone at the corner of the apron on Stage Left and nodded in his direction. "When you done singing, *whatchu* going do until your next set?"

She shrugged. "Get changed. I have a good half hour, maybe forty minutes before I'm due back on stage for the next set."

He grinned at her. "Stay and dance for me. Like old times, *K?*"

"You're just doing this to make him suffer, aren't you?"

"*Everyone like see you dance.* You got one *killah* way of

swaying your hips." Kaleo laughed as loud as he could with the show going on. *"Why not make him pay? 'Sides, you look good in that mu'u. He going swallow his tongue."*

She shoved him back with a playful push of her hand and managed to school her expression from laughter to a gracious smile as she stepped out onto the stage to Mackie's generous introduction.

Hi`ilani walked over to him and took his hand.

At his urging she made a bow that looked more like a curtsy and the audience burst into applause in anticipation.

As she stood back up she took a good look at her mentor.

Mackie had been her teacher, her Kumu Hula, when she was a little girl, taking a real interest in her talent and her education. And through the years, he'd developed that talent and inspired her to sing and learn to play the ukulele and the guitar.

When he handed her the microphone she saw him turn to leave.

"Hold on, Mackie," she chided him with a big smile, "don't run off yet." She held out her free hand and he walked closer and held her hand in his, the stage lights glimmering over the fabric of his vintage suit-coat.

Hi`ilani turned to look at the audience. "Mackie has been my inspiration for most of my life. He's an amazing performer in his own right, but he gives all of his time and effort to help discover, train, and promote young artists in Hawaiian music and dance.

"I'd like to ask you to help me acknowledge the true treasure on the stage tonight. Tommy Mackie!"

She turned off her microphone and led the audience in a round of applause.

Tommy was trying to wave it off, brush away the adoration of the crowd. He gave her a look that said he loved her just as much as it said he was going to give her a stern talking to later.

She pressed a kiss to her fingers and blew it toward him as he walked sideways toward the wings.

Once he stepped into the shadows, she turned the microphone back on and set it in the stand waiting for her at the center of the stage.

The lights were still on in the audience, a favor she'd asked of the lightboard operator. She quickly scanned the audience as she moved down toward the edge of the apron.

"Tonight, I'm starting with a song that Mackie knows well," she spared a glance for the audience as a whole, "and most of you as well. A song about the stars and brown eyes…"

She continued to speak, knowing the words to say since she'd said them over and over again, show after show, but her eyes were only on one person.

Jackson.

She saw him in the audience.

He was taller than most of the people around him, save for two men sitting near him in his row, but she couldn't really focus on them.

Seeing Jackson again was like that first breath of air after diving down into the water and searching the sea floor for shells and pretty pieces of smooth glass. That gulp of air that burns as much as it restores the air.

He was gorgeous, achingly so.

And he'd once been hers.

She saw the look in his eyes, the hope and worry that seemed to war with the other and she said a little prayer that the same look wasn't fixed on her face too.

She thought she'd started to work him out of her system, but she'd been wrong, so very wrong. All she could do was hope that Jackson was here because he thought he'd been wrong too.

It killed him to sit there, watching her.

Oh, it wasn't her performance that made things awkward.

No. In fact, in the time that they had been apart, she had become a better performer when she'd already been amazing to watch.

When she began the song, strumming the strings of the ukulele she'd picked up from the stand beside her, joining a guitar player who sat with the rest of the stage band, the whole room hushed around them.

The few glowing phone screens that he'd seen intermittently around the room turned off or were lowered down.

The audience listened as she sung with a longing in her voice that called to all of them, making it all the more difficult for him.

He'd known that voice.

She'd whispered into his ear in the late-night darkness

of her bedroom. He'd heard her gasp and sigh in his arms. Felt her murmur against his lips.

And he'd lost that.

Given it up.

But he was going to get it back.

He just had to convince Hi`ilani that forgiving him was going to be worth it.

CHAPTER 3

What a rush. Hi`ilani rushed up the stairs to her dressing room. The Old Hawaii Theater had several floors of dressing rooms in the stage right wing that looked like a tenement from West Side Story. The rooms were small-ish but all of them were just perfect as far as she was concerned.

Performing with Kaleo had been like old times, except they weren't wearing t-shirts and jeans and sipping on sodas in between songs. They were friends as well as contemporaries of each other and it showed on stage, which is probably why she stayed for more than one dance, singing along with him on an old romantic song that they'd sung back in their Brown Bags to Stardom days.

And now… she had to rush.

Her second set was still due to start in ten minutes and she had to change her clothes. Tugging on the waist and hips of her long body hugging mu`umu`u and raised it up high enough that she could reach a hand over her shoulder and grasp the zipper pull.

With a little grunt and a little huff she managed to pull it down enough to shrug out of the gown. A quick step out of the garment and she was able to lay it over the back of her chair and reach for the next gown in the rack. Another stylized gown of red with a black pattern of falling kukui leaves was her second and final gown of the night. The wide scoop neckline of the gown set it on the edge of her shoulders and descending down to the near floor-length hem and back into the short train at the back.

She was going to debut one of her own songs in the second set and then end with a cover of *Ku`u Home O Kahalu`u.* That song always felt like it was coming from her soul, the loss of an innocence in her heart when she had to walk away from her first, and what she felt was her true love. So it was strangely apropos that she was set to perform the song with Jackson in the audience.

She shivered as she smoothed her hand up her bare arm. Hi`ilani had told herself time and time again that she was over him and now she couldn't deny that she'd been lying to herself.

Needing a little bit of fresh air she moved to the windows at the back of the dressing room. A few circles of the handle had the window cracked open enough to feel the difference.

And it allowed her to see the park next to the theater. In the day it was a pretty park with a pond and a turtle statue, but at night, the shadows that fell across the park gave it a dangerous look.

She heard a few cars rush along Bethel Street and she turned to look as someone honked. Thank goodness that she'd closed the changing room door behind her or the noise would have gone straight into the stage area and out into the audience.

A soft metallic squeak sounded below her, followed by a soft thud. It wasn't unusual for someone to go outside. Stagehands and performers were known to take a smoke break every once in a while. Curious, she looked down and was surprised to see the wall lamp catch on Mackie's distinctive suit coat. It looked like diamonds in the light, tiny little chips of some kind of reflective material had been worked into the fabric. That jacket had been part of his onstage presence since the 60s.

She almost called out to him, but she looked at the clock and saw that she had five minutes to spare.

She wanted him to know ahead of time that Jackson was in the audience. He'd likely come backstage after the show and given the last time that Mackie had seen Jackson, he'd given him a rather large piece of his mind.

Sliding her feet into her slippers she left her dressing room and headed down the flight of stairs to the ground floor. A quick wave at a stagehand, and she was out the door.

She didn't hear or see anything at first.

"Mackie?"

Still nothing.

Pursing her lips together she turned on her heel to go back inside.

"You leave me out of this."

She stopped short.

The voice had been an echo. She knew it was Mackie and it was outside, but she hadn't seen him.

Turning back around she narrowed her eyes to look deeper into the shadows of the park. A large over-hanging tree made everything seem darker. "Mackie?" She whispered into the dark. "What's going on?"

"You got into this trouble all by yourself, old man. We've given you enough time to square things up. Now we want what you owe us."

She heard the words.

Heard the scuffle of sound.

Looking around she didn't see anyone on the street.

They were a block away from the Chinatown Police Substation. Where was everyone?

A soft groan of pain punctuated a soft thump.

Tears sprung to her eyes as she struggled to understand what was happening.

She wanted… no, she needed to find Mackie and get him inside where there were other people.

Safety in numbers. That's what people always said.

And from the voices she heard. The numbers were against Mackie.

Hi`ilani took a few steps toward the door before she heard another few thumps of sound. When Mackie cried out and began to beg, she knew she couldn't leave him alone out there with whoever was hurting him.

He'd stood by her for years and she was going to stand by him.

Once she found him.

The audience knew something was going on. The end of one act had rolled easily into the next all night, but now the stage was empty.

Jackson turned when Mary put her hand on his arm.

She leaned in and gave him a wink. "How did you ever let that girl go?"

He looked back at her and didn't really have an answer.

After seeing the two couples and knowing that their entire unit was happily living their lives and doing their missions flawlessly he had no answer for her. Nothing that made sense, anyway.

Rayne leaned forward and gave him a disbelieving look. "Her voice is incredible! And the way she dances," she leaned against Ghost's arm and sighed, "I understand what people say about hula. They really tell a story with their movements."

Truck chuckled low in his chest. "The way someone described it to me before we left, I was expecting it to be more like a mime."

Jackson nodded, his eyes straying to the stage. "I didn't know what to expect at my first show either. It didn't take me long to appreciate the art in it."

Truck picked up Mary's hand in his and brought it to his lips. "When you've got the right woman at your side, it really changes the way you see things."

Jackson blew out a breath. "Yeah," he leaned to the side and bumped his arm against the man sitting beside them. "Sorry, sir," he offered the apology, "I was just trying to see backstage."

The man waved if off. "Not a problem, son. Sounds like you know someone in the cast?"

He cleared his throat. "Yes, sir."

Jackson might have said more if he hadn't seen the curtains move at the side of the stage.

A group had gathered in the wings and there were enough voices in the mix to make the sound nearly audible in the house.

He saw Kaleo push through the group to talk to the stage manager and that's when he moved.

He had no way of knowing what was going on.

Not really.

It was just a feeling, deep down in the pit of his stomach.

He barely managed to mutter an, "Excuse me," as he moved to the end of the row and started up the aisle.

The conversation continued and right before he reached the apron on the stage Kaleo looked over in his direction.

Something was wrong and it had to do with Hi`ilani. He'd had a feeling when Mackie hadn't come out on stage to do her introduction.

And he knew her well enough to know that she'd come out anyway if something had prevented Mackie from coming out on stage, because 'the show must go on.'

He jogged up the steps at the side of the stage and none of the stage hands tried to stop him.

Panic.

He felt it nagging at the edges of his calm.

When things went bad on a mission, they had plans

based on plans based on plans. But there was nothing to prepare him for this kind of situation.

Once he was at the corner of the stage he looked around, assessing the situation.

The majority of the staff and cast were gathered in the wings of stage left, crowded near the front of the fly rail. Their voices were getting louder, but he didn't need to hear their words, he saw it all in Kaleo's face. He knew the man enough to know that he wasn't above messing with him because of what he'd done, but the expression on his face told a different story.

She wouldn't be in her dressing room. That would have been checked already. The other usual places, too.

A soft bump of sound off to the left turned his head.

The side door to the park was open.

That struck him as odd. He'd been in the building before and had heard the warnings. That door had to remain closed to keep out the homeless that sometimes inhabited the park from time to time.

That was a place to start.

Pushing his way out of the door, he closed it quietly behind him.

Sorting through the sounds of the city around him, he searched for the one sound he needed to hear. Her voice.

The pond in the park wasn't natural. The city had spent a chunk of money installing a pump system that looked like it was a big rock pile.

That's where she figured the sounds had to come from, the dark side of that installation.

Just a few weeks ago there had been a restaurant open on the far side of the pond and that would have made it impossible to hide back there with a bunch of patio tables just a foot or two away, but now it was only too clear how dangerous this whole area was now.

Dark enough to make people invisible to prying eyes.

She felt the rocks before she expected to. She jammed her toes into the rough surface and barely held back a cry of pain.

"I'll get you your money. I just need more time."

A rough grunt was followed by a withering moan.

They were hurting him!

"No more, please. I already promised you-"

Hi`ilani moved forward, her mind furiously working over her options, or the lack of them. She had to do something.

And soon.

"And you don't have the money, so your promises are no good. Are they?"

The metallic click that echoed in the quiet night air pushed her forward and the rock she was circling tore her gown.

The sound of the rip sounded like a scream in the darkness and that was enough to startle everyone.

"Who came out here with you?"

"No one," Mackie groaned, "I came alone. Like you said."

"We need to go! If someone's out there-"

"We'll take him with us and get the cash."

"Fine," Mackie sounded like he was crying, "take me with you. I won't fight."

He'd given up. Mackie sounded like he wanted to die.

That was unacceptable.

She wasn't going to let that happen.

"Don't! Please!" She rushed toward the voices and stopped when she saw a gun pointed right at her. "Let him go."

"You brave or stupid, girl?"

Holding her hands out in front of her, she tried to get a look at Mackie, but he was deep in the shadows. Only the ghost of a glimmer from his jacket was visible in the faint light of the security light from the abandoned restaurant.

"Stupid," she told them. "I'm stupid, but Mackie's my friend. Please let him go. I won't tell anyone about-"

A door banged open behind her and the world stopped spinning.

The soft lapping sounds of the pond turned into a heavy slush of sound. The two men before her froze and then burst into sluggish movements.

Mackie was pulled into the light, his face contorted into a mask of fear... for her.

The men were mad, blaming Mackie for a double cross, but she couldn't seem to speak or move. She just stood there with her arms in front of her, lost in the most terrifying moment of her life.

She heard footsteps pounding across the pavement behind her.

Help was coming.

She knew that.

"Damn Bitch!"

She heard a metallic click and her eyes lifted. There were two guns pointed at her now.

And two men moving away from her, toward the far side of the park.

She felt the first few pangs of hope that everything was going to be okay. If they were moving away. They weren't planning to shoot

And she smiled.

Smiled at Mackie.

So that he'd know everything was going to be fine.

"Someone's got to pay!"

"No!"

She told herself to move. Told her legs to move. She should have been able to do something.

But Mackie did.

He pulled himself free and turned.

"Get down!" Someone behind her was shouting, repeating the order again, but she kept her eyes on Mackie.

That's why she saw it happen.

Both guns exploded at the same time. She was sure she felt the concussion of the shots, but it was only when Mackie fell into her that she began to drop.

She wrapped both arms around him to cushion his fall and lifted her face to look at the men in disbelief.

One at a time they passed under the streetlight at the other end of the park and she saw them. Saw their faces.

It was probably only for a moment, but that moment seemed to last forever for her.

Until everything went black.

Blood.

Shit. There was so much damn blood.

Jackson heard Ghost's command and was more than eager to follow it. He dropped down to the cement beside Hi`ilani and Mackie.

He found pulses for both and called the information over his shoulder. One of the women answered back. Someone was on a cell phone with 911. The rest of it was just noise.

Someone must have turned on the flood lights because the whole park was suddenly lit up like it was daytime.

Mackie groaned and tried to move, but Jackson put a steadying hand on his shoulder. "You're shot. Let me help you."

The two wounds were easily visible on the back of his jacket. The flood lights only made it look garish and horrifying. Mackie wasn't a big man and the shots had drilled through his back.

"I don't... don't think they went through."

Gingerly, Jackson rolled Mackie to the side so he could see between them.

There was blood on her arms where she'd wrapped them around Mackie during their fall. He'd seen that much. There was no blood on her dress, no sign that she had been shot as well. He began to peel off his jacket.

"No," he told the older man, "you saved her."

A soft laugh coughed from his lips and bubbles of blood burst from his mouth and popped against his chin and cheeks. "She... saved me."

Sirens blared out into the night, cutting through the excited murmurs of the gathering crowd.

"Ambulance is coming." Jackson gave him a smile. "Hold on." Quickly folding his jacket, he placed it against Mackie's back to staunch the flow of blood.

Mackie's next breath wheezed from his throat. "Don't bother." Another cough, weaker this time. "Tell her… that I'm sorry."

"For what?" Jackson leaned down, trying to catch Mackie's eye.

"Move aside, sir. Emergency Services."

He wanted to argue and ask Mackie the question again. Instead his training took over and he rattled off the observations he'd kept fresh in his head.

One EMT worked on each of them at the site, calling out observations to the other while they worked.

Movement from the other side of the park drew his eyes for a moment.

Ghost and Truck were back, empty handed. China-town was a maze of dark entries and back alleys. Criminals who worked the streets likely knew every little nook and cranny. He turned back to the scene and felt a gentle hand touch his arm.

Rayne leaned in closer, her voice reaching his ear easily. "What happened?"

"She hit her head, but she wasn't shot. I don't think Mackie's going to make it."

As they all gathered together, Jackson kept his focus on both of them as the EMTs examined the two. His hands itched and he looked down at them, there was drying blood on his right hand, left over from trying to stop the flow of Mackie's blood.

"Here," Rayne handed him a packet of wipes, murmuring, "I've gotten used to carrying them around with all the crazy stuff that happens."

Truck reached out and pulled Mary into his arms as the EMT working on Hi`ilani turned to look up at Jackson. "We'll need to take him in first. They can send another ambulance for her in a few minutes."

Jackson crouched down beside her and smoothed his hand over her face, quietly speaking to her. "Hey, hey… I need you to wake up."

Her eyes fluttered open and she started, jerking away from his hand.

"You're okay." He reached out a gentle hand to touch her, but she pulled away, pushing up onto her hands as she looked around at the unfamiliar faces beside him, her eyes widening in confusion. He tried to draw her attention back to him so she wouldn't see the EMTs. "They're sending another ambulance and-"

Another.

She mouthed the word and turned.

The two EMTs seemed frozen in time. Sitting still as statues until one lifted his head to look at the other.

All it took was a subtle head shake and the world fell apart.

"No." Hi`ilani got up on her knees, but she couldn't stand. The long length of her gown was caught up with her legs. The EMTs lifted Mackie's still form onto the gurney. She reached out a hand. "No, wait!"

The EMT on the far side of the gurney gave her an apologetic look. "We're sorry, miss."

"No, no… you can't stop trying. Just get him to the hospital."

Jackson helped her to her feet, but he had a feeling she didn't even know what he was doing.

The other EMT reached down to the base of the gurney and lifted the edge of the sheet.

"No, no! Please don't. Not him. Not him." She reached out a hand toward them and froze.

Some of the blood on her hands was still wet, glistening between her fingers.

Jackson wrapped his arms closer around her body. "Babe, don't look."

"Oh my God!"

She turned her hand in one direction and then the other. The pale glow of the street light cast enough light to make her skin sallow and the blood a glossy red-black that made Jackson's skin crawl.

And he'd seen his share of blood.

When the EMTs turned away to roll the gurney toward the ambulance, she came to life again. Lurching forward, one of her feet stomped on the toe of his shoe. She was light enough that he didn't really notice it.

All he could do was hold onto her as she started to cry… and scream… and beg.

It was the begging that did it.

Tears swam in his eyes as he heard her begging them to try again. To try something else.

"Me!" She pounded her open hand against her chest. "It was supposed to be me!"

"Baby, stop."

She tried to push away from him, free herself from his restraining hold, but he didn't let her.

"They did everything they could-"

"Don't!" Hi`ilani turned on him. She brought her hands up between them and shoved at him with her palms. "Don't say that! He'll be fine. He will! They just can't give up... no, no!" She started to turn around again, but he lowered his arms to her lower back, pulling her closer against his body.

Her arms were loose but he didn't care.

She pounded at his shoulders, raining blows down on him as she struggled in his embrace, but he didn't let go.

Not when the ambulance pulled away.

Not when the police tried to speak to her.

Not even when she wore herself out, her hands dropping listlessly to her side and her voice wore down into a rough whisper.

He didn't let go.

Jackson figured he'd done enough of that in the past. From now on, he was going to make it up to her. No matter what it took.

CHAPTER 4

She was surprised when Jackson just took her exactly where she said she wanted to go. Maybe he was giving her a break. The last day certainly hadn't done her any favors, turning what should have been the happiest day in her life into the worst.

The police detective had followed them to Queen's Hospital and questioned her in the examination room. She knew Jackson wanted to argue with the timing, there was no mistaking the angry clench of his jaw and the tight tick of a muscle in his cheek.

From there, they'd gone to the police station, the main HPD office on Beretania Street was just no more than two blocks away. Officer Wong had started her on the mug shots in the computer and switched to physical pictures when her eyes blurred and her headache got worse.

She knew Jackson had wanted to leave, but she had to stay. If she could find the men in the books then they could arrest them.

She owed that to Mackie.

Owed her life to him.

Jackson opened the passenger door of his Jeep and lifted her down to the ground. She would have argued in the past, but she was too tired to do anything more than push her hand into her purse and grab her keys.

He walked her to her door and stood there with his hand on her lower back as she tried to grab hold of the key for the front door.

She'd tried a handful of times before he gently pulled the ring from her fingers and held it out.

"Which key?"

She lifted her head and looked him in the eyes. "Green."

He flipped through the keys and separated the key with the green plastic tag on it. "Okay. Let's get you inside."

The grating sound of metal against metal actually settled her nerves. Made it easier for her to just blank out her mind. Ignore the aching empty spot in her chest that seemed to extend down into her soul.

The screen door swung out and he used the advantage of his height to pull it to the side without making her duck. He didn't even have to look at her or ask the question again. She just told him. "Pink."

Jackson swung the heavy wooden door open a few seconds later and she stepped inside.

She didn't have to turn around to know that he'd closed the door behind them. Jackson had a presence that was impossible to miss, like he was able to fill up the room around her like a physical touch.

It was too tempting to walk into his arms and stay there forever.

She had to put some distance between them. Reaching out, she put her hand on the top of her tiny dining room table. Her hands were clean. She'd washed them half a dozen times at the emergency room and then again before they'd left the police station.

Still, she knew what had been on them just a few hours ago and she felt like she could probably wash them a hundred times more and she would still feel the blood wet between her fingers, or flaking off the back of her hands.

"Do you think I should go back in the morning and look at the photos again?"

She heard the soft chime of the keys on a hard surface.

"You looked over all of them tonight."

Hi`ilani nodded. "But only one of the men was in there. Or at least I think it was one of them. If one is in there… shouldn't the other one be in there too?"

The room remained silent as she remembered Officer Wong's words when he'd sat her down with the computer as they began the search. "These are only the photos of the men we've had in custody before. One, or both of the men, might not be in here. If they're new to the game or if they just haven't been taken into custody before, you may not see them."

And that was likely true.

The one picture that she believed that she'd recognized had only been because she'd covered half of the photo with her hand and squinted at it.

Trying to be a witness to a crime committed in the

long shadows of a nearly abandoned park wasn't going to make it easy.

Or even possible.

"You should get some sleep."

His words made sense.

"I'm exhausted," she swallowed and tapped her finger-tips on the table top, "but I'm too wired to sleep." Her eyes closed for a split second before they snapped open again and she felt the underlying tension between them like a tremor under her feet.

Turning back toward the door, she looked at Jackson and lost her emotional footing.

"You came to the show tonight."

He nodded slowly.

"Looks like I made a hell of an impression on your friends." Her cheeks heated up with shame. "I'm sorry I lost my mind back there. I think I remember most of what I did, but I think I'm just so numb…"

"Numb happens."

She heard sympathy in his voice, understanding.

"And then the pain is going to hit you. Over and over. Sometimes it's going to be a little twinge of pain in your chest. And then when you least expect it, it might knock you to your knees and steal your breath."

"You know I lost my mom when I was younger," she didn't wait for his reaction, they'd spoken about her mother's death when they were together before, "but that was in a hospice, quiet and calm. And you're probably speaking from experience. When you were deployed overseas, right?"

A quick nod was the answer she needed.

"Someone took Mackie from me. No one is ever going to replace him in my life. He believed in me from the very beginning and it was really starting to pay off. I had something I wanted to tell him tonight." There it was, that twinge of grief in her chest, as if someone had reached in and squeezed her heart. "I was going to wait until we were done so we could go and celebrate together."

And we'll never have another moment like that again.

Her breath burst from her lips and pulled back in on a gasping sob. "Oh God, he's gone."

She felt herself falling, knew she couldn't stop herself in time.

But when the ground didn't rush up underneath her she felt his arms around her again, his hand cradling the back of her head and gently guiding it to lean against his shoulder.

It felt so good to be in his arms. To hear the reassuring beat of his heart in his chest.

"It feels like it's been forever," she murmured against his shirt, rubbing her cheek against the soft cotton.

She felt him place a kiss on the top of her head and the hand on her back smoothed slowly up and down her backbone as he cuddled her close.

"It feels like nothing's changed."

A shudder ran through her from head to toe, but she didn't move away from him. It was just too tempting to enjoy the warmth and comfort that he offered. "Is that what it feels like?"

She knew her voice was barely a whisper, but that was all she could manage with her heart lodged in her throat.

"Is that why you came to the show?" She was glad that

she wasn't looking up at him. She didn't know what she wanted to see in his face, but she also didn't want to be disappointed.

"I came because I wanted to tell you that I was wrong."

Breathe. She told herself to breathe.

She was already walking the edge of grief, fighting off her tears.

"I was wrong when I told you it couldn't work, that I couldn't see you anymore."

Light headed.

She felt light headed.

"I think I need to sit down."

She expected him to let her go. To let her fold down onto the couch behind her.

Moments later she found herself seated across his lap, leaning back against the padded arm of the couch. It was a rush, yes, but it also stole her breath.

He took her hand in his and covered it so that he gave her his warmth. "I need to explain what happened, but you need to know that there's one part of this that you can't mention to anyone."

"What do you mean, I can't tell anyone? What can't I tell them?"

"What I have to tell you has to stay between you and me whether you decide you can forgive me, or not." She watched his lips press into a thin white line and saw his eyes darken. "Can you do that, Hi`ilani? Can you keep my secret?" She saw him swallow, his Adam's apple rising and falling under his skin. "Can you promise me just this one thing?"

She could hear the worry in his tone and saw the

concern in his eyes. "What's wrong, Jack? You're scaring me."

Jackson shook his head. "I'm sorry, baby. You've had a hell of a night and if I'd done the right thing before you wouldn't have to go through this now. I just need you to give me this chance to explain."

"Okay," she let a breath sigh from her lips, "tell me."

He was trained to focus. Heartrate down, focus up.

He was trained to infiltrate enemy strongholds, extract innocents, government employees, and prisoners of war.

He was trained to light 'em up and take 'em down.

But sitting there on Hi`ilani's couch he felt like he was about to jump headlong into a rushing river with swollen banks. He had to swim or sink.

And damn it, he wanted to swim.

"That training that I went to," the first thing he did was hit rough water, there were so many ways he could finish that sentence and none of them sounded or felt good, so he went for the embarrassing truth, "right before I made an ass of myself, was actually a selection and was supposed to be kept as secret as everything else I couldn't tell you back then." He felt her tug on her hand, but he didn't let go. Jackson kept his hands gentle. "It was a selection for Delta Force."

He could tell by the look in her eyes that she didn't know what that meant.

"First Special Forces Operational Detachment-Delta. They call it Delta Force, but what it all boils down to is that we're a special mission unit for the Army, like the SEAL Teams are for the Navy."

Her eyes narrowed and she wiggled a little to sit up higher against the arm of the sofa. "Delta Force? There were movies about that, right?"

He nodded, chuckling softly. "Yeah. There were some movies, but it's more than that."

"Oh, I get it," she smiled for the first time since they'd left the theater. "I'm just sorry I don't understand what this had to do with anything."

"Deltas, like the SEALS, we don't tell people what we do. Secrecy is what keeps us alive both in the field and at home.

"Part of that secrecy is keeping our interactions to a minimum."

The look in her eyes told him he'd stepped in something.

"Interactions? Well that sounds clinical. Are you sure you're not a doctor? That would be a little less aggravating."

He lifted one hand away and rubbed at his forehead. "I thought this through more than a dozen times before I even got to the theater, but I'm still sticking my foot in my mouth."

"Pretty much."

He hung his head for a moment, trying to organize his thoughts, but as soon as he untangled one the others tied themselves up in knots. He wanted to give up, let her go to sleep, talk later when he'd had a chance to think it through another hundred times or so.

Right.

He was never going to get it right.

And then she touched him.

Set her hand on the back of his neck.

Brushed her thumb along his skin and sent shivers down his spine.

"Jack."

She moved her thumb again, brushing back in the other direction. He would sit there forever as long as she kept touching him.

"Jack, look at me."

He turned his head, but didn't move anything else. He was selfish enough to want her hands on him.

"I'm trying to understand, Jack. It's just been a long day. Please, just tell me what you're thinking."

It wasn't until he blew out his breath between his barely parted lips that he realized he'd been holding it in.

"I'm thinking that you're so beautiful it makes me ache just to look at you. That when you touch me, I don't ever want you to stop.

"You need to know that if I didn't think… didn't believe that it was the best thing for you that I stayed away, I wouldn't have done it."

He still had a hold of her hand, and brought it up to his lips and then leaned his cheek against the backs of her fingers.

"We could be called up for a mission with barely enough time to get to the hangar. We could be gone for days, weeks, who knows. And if something were to happen to us, all the Army could tell our next of kin was that we died. Things that we see and do have to remain a secret for everyone outside of our unit and our command.

Families, we were told, were a luxury that we wouldn't be able to enjoy

"And then I met Truck and Ghost, the two men I was with at the theater. They belong to a Delta Force team based in Texas. My commander asked me to meet with them and answer any questions they had about what to do while they're here and while we talked, I met their wives.

"That's what floored me. Wives and some of the men in their unit have children. And here I thought I'd given all of that up when they selected me to become a Delta. The first thing I wanted to do was tell you. Talk to you and explain that I was wrong when I told you I couldn't see you anymore."

He watched as she processed his words. At least she wasn't telling him to get out. That had to mean something.

"So…" she pulled her lower lip between her teeth and worried it for a moment, "you came to apologize for what you said."

"Yeah." He pressed a kiss to the back of her hand. "That was something I owed you, but there was more to it than that."

She sat there, waiting, with her eyes fixed on his face.

He could say so many things to her, he could try to explain, but there was one thing he really needed her to hear.

"I love you. I loved you then, but I didn't want you to have to worry about me when I was called away. I thought it would be better for you if I made it a clean break and walked way.

"Looking back now I realize that I was a complete

idiot and up until the shooting last night my intent was to get down on my knees and beg your forgiveness, to give me a chance to be in your life again, but now…"

Her eyes were shining with tears and he worried that he might have crossed the line with her.

"I don't want you to make a decision or even worry about this until later. You need some sleep."

"Sleep?" She shook her head. "You tell me you're part of some secret special missions team and that's why you broke my heart. You tell me you love me and you want me to let you back into my life." She took in a breath that sounded like a gasp. "But you think I can just go right to sleep?"

"You need to get some rest."

"And you need to not drop a bomb in my lap and expect me to shrug it off. I'm still trying to understand even half of what you've said to me, Jack."

She pulled her hand away from his and used her other hand to push against the back of the sofa as she dropped her legs to the floor.

"Well the good news is that I'm so exhausted that I'm going to try to sleep. So you can go whenever you want. I guess I'll see how I feel about it in the morning."

He stood as she moved toward the doorway. He didn't know what was beyond it, but he wasn't about to invite himself further into her home.

When she was gone out of his sight he waited right where he was standing. He'd made a tactical error with her.

Again.

He could plan any kind of mission and get his team in

and out safely, but talking to the woman he loved? Total FUBAR. Maybe he wasn't cut out for a relationship after all.

But Hi`ilani? She made him desperate to try.

He heard water turn on. A sink by the sounds of it. He stood there waiting while she washed up, opened drawers, and probably changed her clothes.

He didn't move.

Couldn't.

Not yet.

Not even when she stepped back through the doorway and stood there watching him as she rolled one foot over so that her toes were curled under, making the arch in her foot really noticeable.

"You're still here."

He nodded. "And I'm planning to stay." Jackson gestured at the sofa. "I'll sit here through the night."

She squinted at the windows that lined the front of her apartment. "It's almost dawn."

"And through the rest of the day until we've heard from the police that they've caught the men who tried to shoot you."

"That could be days, Jack!"

"Then I'll stay for days."

"But you've got your missions to do with your team, right?"

"We're on leave. All of us. I've got time. And anytime your life is in danger, I'd take leave again, in a heartbeat."

He could see the moment she just gave up arguing, but it was also the moment when he could see just how exhausted she was.

"Go to sleep, Hi`ilani. I'll stay out here." He saw the way she closed her eyes, squeezing them tight to hold back her tears. "I won't let anyone get to you. You have my word on that."

Stepping away from the wall she started to back up and go back the way she came.

He watched her as she mulled through her thoughts. He didn't move. She needed to think things through without him pushing for the outcome he wanted.

"Jack?"

When she spoke, he could hear the uncertainty in her voice. He just didn't know whether that was a good thing or not. But damn it, he wanted to find out.

"Yeah?"

She started forward and before he knew it, she had her arms wrapped around his waist. Leaning her cheek against his chest she held him tightly as she shook from head to toe.

He felt her tears wetting the front of his shirt and he didn't care one bit.

Jackson wrapped his arms around her and held her gently as she cried, pressing little kisses on the top of her head as she held onto him.

He had no idea about how long it lasted, and would have been happy to let it continue as long as she needed him.

Holding her was heaven, feeling her pain and knowing he couldn't do a thing to stop it, was absolute hell.

When she stopped shaking she loosened her hold on him and stepped back.

He reluctantly let her go, but this was not the time to

do what he wanted. She needed to know that he was there for her.

She looked up at him and there was the slightest smile touching her lips. "There's something you should know, Jack. Something I wanted to tell you almost a year ago, right before… before you walked away."

Jackson waited for her to continue. He wasn't going to say a word until she had her say.

"I loved you, Jack. I know I didn't have a clue about your job and what all that entails. All I knew was that you were in the Army. And that you were one of the best men I'd ever known. Then you broke my heart and I'm not sure if I can feel that way about you again." She closed her lips and swallowed, wringing her hands together once and then again. "Seeing you again, feeling the way you hold me, makes me feel like it's possible, but I'm just so confused. And I'm tied up in knots."

She closed her eyes and he watched her carefully. Just in case she needed him again.

"So I'm going to try to get some sleep. And while I know I won't be able to convince you to leave, there's a part of me that doesn't want you to. I don't have anything for you to change into and I'm sorry."

He tilted his head toward the door. "I have a bag in my car with a change of clothes. "I'll wait until you're in bed before I go out and get it. Good night, Hi`ilani. *Aloha ahiahi.*"

Her whole face changed, smoothing away the deep worry lines from the last few hours. Her smile softened and her eyes crinkled up at the corners. "*Aloha ahiahi,* Jack."

CHAPTER 5

He came awake and sat up in bed, suddenly alert. It was a skill that he'd developed when he joined the army. You never knew when his superior officers would surprise them with an early wake up or spring something on them in the middle of the night.

It was a skill that had saved his life a number of times during his deployment and on missions.

They'd arrived at night, but after assuring himself that she was sleeping soundly, he'd gone back outside for his bag and to familiarize himself with the layout of her duplex.

In the crush of apartment buildings and hotels in Waikiki, he was surprised that she'd found a room to rent in a two-story building surrounded by much taller buildings.

The landscaping was good. The bushes weren't overly thick or tall so the windows still received their share of light, but wouldn't offer too much of a shield if someone were trying to look in through the windows.

Still, the ground floor had its advantages and disadvantages, but what bothered him the most were the jalousie windows. It limited the ability to evacuate should the need arise.

Lifting up a hand, he scratched at the back of his neck and looked over at Hiʻilani, asleep beside him.

It wasn't how they'd gone to bed.

He'd been happy to sleep on the couch. He'd slept in worse places and it was a luxury to sleep on something with at least a little give.

But that hadn't lasted for more than an hour.

That was when her nightmares started.

The early morning sounds of traffic outside the windows had its own unique patterns, punctuated by single cars here and there dashing through the lanes at their own speed.

But he heard one of those oddities rush past the bedroom window, but then the quick left turn had him swinging his legs down to the floor.

It was a one-way street like so many others in Waikiki, but the car had turned and gone down against the flow of traffic.

A few moments later a car door slammed on the street and Jackson was on his feet. Alert. On guard. He'd picked up his gun from the bedside table and slipped it into the back of his waistband.

The gun's weight made the pants hang low on his hips, but fashion wasn't his concern. Never really had been.

One last look at Hiʻilani where she lay resting peacefully for the first time in the last few hours, he moved into the front room.

The louvered window covering gave him a good look at an HPD cruiser parked haphazardly along the curb. And the flash of dark blue uniform beside the door said that either they were getting an official visit, or someone was at least making the pretext of a cover.

He wasn't going to take any chances.

More banging at the door. "Open the door, Lani. We've got to talk."

The man was careless. He didn't even bother trying to look in through the windows. Jackson bent down just enough to look up through the tilted frosted-glass louvers and took a good look at the man's face, memorizing it.

"Damn it, Lani! You can't hide from me!"

That's it.

Jackson yanked open the heavy wooden door.

Staring at the officer through the screen door, he shot a glance to the name tag.

"Officer Ballard?"

"Who are you?"

"I'm the guy you just pissed off. You should turn around and head back to your cruiser. You have no business here."

The officer was apparently not in the mood to follow orders.

Taking a step back, he looked back at Jackson through the screen.

"I'm not leaving until I see Lani."

The way he said her name, or part of her name as the case may be, really crawled over Jackson's nerves.

"She's asleep and dead tired. You're going to leave and when she wants to call you, she'll call you."

Jackson wondered what kind of a medal he should get for being as diplomatic as he'd been.

And still, the officer stood there. With his dark blond hair and his athletic build, Jackson thought he was probably a surfer in his off hours.

But it was the dark eyes that glared at him that got even further under his own skin.

"You're still here, Officer."

"I'm not leaving until I see Lani, so you can take your orders and shove them-"

"I'm awake."

Jackson looked back over his shoulder and saw her standing in the arch of the open doorway. He muttered under his breath. "Sorry."

She shrugged and leaned against the door frame for a moment before she moved again, a yawn making her first step a stumble.

"You should go back to bed. I can deal with him."

When she looked up through the screen Jackson did too and neither of them missed the angry glare on the officer's face.

"What is it, Kyle?"

"Let me in, Lani."

She shook her head. "Not today. I can't talk to you today."

Jackson heard the little catch in her voice, but Kyle seemed to be oblivious to it.

"I heard about Mackie, babe. I wanted to be here for you."

Babe.

It took everything in Jackson not to tell the man where to step off.

Was he seeing Hi`ilani?

He hadn't asked her the night before if she was seeing anyone.

"I just got back from the police station a few hours ago." Her voice was soft and her eyes were still red-rimmed from her tears, but she stood tall and met the officer straight in the eyes. She never had been a shrinking violet. "I'm really tired."

"Then I'll stay here with you. The captain said I could have the rest of the shift off if you need me."

Jackson's back teeth ground against each other. He wanted to tell the man to shove his suggestion where the sun doesn't shine but this wasn't his apartment. And right now, he still wasn't back in her life.

Yet.

Jackson focused on her face. "What would you like?"

The question staggered her enough to make her tilt her head in his direction. "Wow. You want to know what I think?"

"I always did. I just wanted to protect you more."

The huffing sound that came through the screen was a little less than civil. "What's going on here?"

Hi`ilani turned to the officer. "Jackson stayed with me after… after… I wasn't in any condition to find my way home."

"Jackson," the officer's tone was barely a snarl, "the army grunt."

Taking a quick moment to look at the officer again, he nodded. "Jarhead?"

There was a light in his eyes visible even through the screen. "Proud of it." Leaning to the side he looked at the back of the room.

Jackson followed his gaze and saw the blanket that he'd left half-on and half-off the couch and the pillow near the arm.

Ballard gave him a smirk. "Why don't you go find your shirt and let me talk to my girlfriend."

If he hadn't seen the drawn look on her face, Jackson would have punched the officer through the screen door. Being an ass over a woman? He'd seen better men than Officer Ballard do the same, but when someone you were supposed to care about goes through something traumatic that's when you stop showing your ass.

"I'll go get my shirt." He said those words to Hi`ilani. "Where do you want me to wait?"

"Wait?" The officer reached for the door and yanked at the handle. "Open the door."

Jackson would have moved at that moment, but Hi`ilani touched her hand to his arm. It was only a little momentary touch, but it was enough.

Enough to stop Jackson in his tracks.

Enough to have the officer seeing red.

"Kyle, stop it!"

Hi`ilani was shaking, her eyes tearing up again.

"Fuck." Jackson reached out and pulled her into his

arms, holding her gently. It was Hi`ilani that wrapped her arms tightly around him.

"I can't…" she shook and rubbed her face against him, making his skin wet, "I just can't argue anymore."

Something rattled the screen door and she only pulled him tighter against her, turning to press her ear against his chest.

Turning his head, Jackson glared at the officer. "Look, I'm not arguing with you here. Neither is she. She's barely slept more than an hour.

"Come back later if you want to talk to her, until then, she really needs some sleep."

He could tell the man wanted to throw him out, grab him by the collar and toss him out into the street. Well, if he had a collar.

But there was something that came over his face that gave Jackson pause. Sure, the guy was an ass of the first kind, but the way Officer Ballard looked at Hi`ilani as she burrowed into Jackson's arms, spoke volumes.

He cared.

And he must have finally decided to show it.

"I'm sorry you lost your friend, Lani. Call me when you get up, okay?"

"Yeah, okay."

Her voice was barely a whisper and Jackson tried to ignore the way his heart tumbled as she held onto him as if the world would turn upside down if he wasn't there for her.

The officer gave Jackson a look that was basically a promise to take him apart piece by piece and then he left.

With a nudge of his hand he swung the wooden door

closed and set the lock. "Hey, why don't you go back to bed."

She looked up at him and took his breath away.

How had he walked away from this woman?

How had he turned his back on what they had together?

Commander Chastain's words infiltrated his thoughts. "It's up to you to protect the ones you love."

In a different context, he'd taken that message to heart and walked away from her.

Now that he had her back in his arms the last thing he wanted to do was let her go.

&a.

She swallowed hard, but the lump in her throat wouldn't go away. Looking up at Jackson, seeing the look in his eyes, it melted her heart.

Made her fight off her tears.

Made her want to hold him tight and listen to his heart.

When she'd gone to sleep, leaving him on the couch, it had been fine. She'd just taken a quick towel-bath and pulled on something to sleep in, pants… shirt.

Pulling the blanket up and over her shoulder, grasping it just under her chin, she'd closed her eyes and managed to fall asleep from exhaustion.

But there wasn't going to be any sweet dreams.

There wasn't even going to be a real restful sleep.

She heard the men shouting.

Heard Mackie pleading.

And then she'd stepped into the whole situation and messed it up.

The yelling. The threats. And then the guns went off.

Mackie stepped in between her and the bullets. He'd given his life to save her.

And that's when she'd started to scream.

And Jackson had been there.

He'd wrapped her up in his arms and let her hold him, let her pound her fists against him, let her cry until his shirt was wet with her tears.

She barely noticed it when he'd pulled it off and used it to dry her face, wipe away the evidence of her tears.

He hadn't let go of her.

Hadn't made her let go of him.

When she laid down and pulled him along with her, he'd laid down beside her and let her listen to his heart until she'd fallen asleep again.

"I'm not ready." She let go of the breath that she'd been holding. "I can't be with you. I just can't. Not right now. I've got… I mean, there's so much-"

"Hey." He leaned forward and pressed a kiss on her forehead. "I love you. I'm not going anywhere." Another kiss eased the tension in her shoulders. "And nothing needs to be decided now. I just want to be here for you if you need me."

She did.

She really did.

And she told herself it was just for the day. Just for that moment.

"Can you hold me?"

She squeezed her eyes shut to keep her tears from falling.

"I'm not saying that I want-"

"I know," he gathered her closer in his arms and whispered into her ear. "I just want to hold you too. I could have lost you before I told you how much you meant to me. I can't think about what could have happened if Mackie hadn't saved you."

Her eyes opened wide, her gaze pierced the popcorn-painted ceiling above her head and the old frosted light-fixture. Everything looked like it was in sharp focus as if she was looking at the world around her like it was a backdrop instead of something three dimensional.

And it was all because she felt his tears.

Against her cheek.

Against the edge of her ear.

He shuddered against her.

Pulled her tighter.

Somehow she found her voice.

"Come to bed, Jack. I need you."

The blankets were already pulled back and when Jackson settled his hand on her lower back she bit back a groan. Just the gentle touch of his fingers a hair above her waistband felt so good. A calming touch that she'd felt a hundred times before.

"Go head," he urged her, "lie down. I'll get the blanket."

She lay down, braced up on an elbow at first, turning over her pillow. She'd cried into it enough before. She didn't want to remember that. Not at that moment.

Laying her head on her pillow she watched as Jackson picked up the blanket from the ground at the foot of the bed and lifted it up and over her feet.

Climbing in beside her, he drew it up and over both of their bodies before letting it go.

She watched his eyes grow darker as his gaze moved over her face.

"I've dreamed of you so many times. Remembered what it was like to fall asleep with you in my arms."

Nodding, she reached out her hand and touched her fingers to his chest. Felt the subtle shift of muscles beneath his skin. "I missed you too."

She sighed when he lifted his hand and brushed his fingers through her hair, trailing his fingertips down her arm, and then he started again.

The gentle touch soothed her nerves.

A clock on the nightstand ticked and changed over to the next hour.

"What time is it?"

Groaning, he looked at the watch on his wrist and sighed. Almost eight a.m. Do you have to be somewhere?"

The question cut through the haze she'd been in and a soft laugh left her lips. "It's amazing how much things can change in less than a day." She lifted her hand and touched the side of his face. "Yesterday morning I was getting ready to teach my kids hula class at the Royal Shopping Center. I had no idea all of the things that would happen later in the day."

"I wish things had turned out differently, too." His hand settled on her hip, his thumb smoothing over her tender flesh. "I wanted to introduce you to my new friends."

She couldn't stop the yawn that filled her lungs and squeezed her eyes shut for a moment. Hi`ilani cuddled in closer to his side. "Are they leaving soon?"

"They're going to be here for another week or so on vacation."

"Maybe." Another yawn and her eyes were barely open, her breathing slower, deeper. "Maybe I can meet them before they go home."

"That sounds like a plan." He continued stroking his thumb over her hip, lulling her slowly to sleep. "Now get some rest. I'm not going to let anything happen to you."

Hotel Street in downtown Honolulu was a dichotomy in culture. Bars that would have to stretch to be considered dives were interspersed with community bakeries, trade schools, art galleries, and tourist shops. To walk along the street one would find themselves mingling with every walk of life from the homeless panhandler sitting in the setback doorway of a closed acupuncturist's office and the lawyers and lawmakers that made their way to hole in the wall eateries.

Sato walked from his penthouse condo across the

busier cross streets until he reached Bethel Street. A quick look to the right made him look like every other weekday gawker interested in the big news story.

Conroy Mackie was a local celebrity. Anyone and everyone in the local performing arts community treated the man like the icon he was.

News that he was gunned down outside of one of his showcases had shaken the downtown area like the San Andreas fault did to California.

When he reached the tattoo parlor at the next corner he caught sight of his face in the glass.

He wore his anger like a dark look, creasing the skin between his brows. He was going to have to stop that, at least until he reached his destination.

Crossing at the light be nodded at one of the policeman on foot. The officer nodded and continued on without really meeting Sato's eyes.

The little mama-San who ran the noodle shop on the corner shrank back from the window when she saw him coming, but that didn't upset him.

A certain amount of fear was healthy, for both his business and the people of Chinatown. When he reached the first bar he pushed open the door and nodded to the bartender. She had green hair today, but he didn't stop to ask her about it. If she wanted to ruin her looks it was fine by him.

He stepped into the back hall and everyone outside, if they were looking in might assume that he was heading for the bathrooms.

But he continued on past the two doors and pushed through another door that said EMPLOYEES ONLY.

When the door swung open, the men inside all looked up. Two of them already had their hands on their guns.

And they were smart enough not to raise them in his presence.

Readiness was good. Being a little too eager was not.

Crossing the room, he watched the girl behind the desk push a button and the door behind him was locked with a deadbolt.

Sato didn't stop to sit at his desk. He went over to the bar and poured himself a glass of vodka.

The bite of the drink as it went down his throat eased some of his anger.

When he set the glass down with a bang he turned and stared at the two men seated on a sofa in the middle of the room.

"You two want to explain why there's police tape up at the park and half a dozen more police on the street?"

The smaller of the two shifted on the chair and shot the other man a glare.

"No?" He sighed. "I'm disappointed. Peck?"

The Caucasian man looked a little odd in the room. Bigger than nearly everyone else, he naturally saw himself in a position of power. "I did what you asked. Billy said he knew where to get to the old man so I went along with his play."

Sato turned his head a fraction of an inch. "Billy?"

The younger man scowled at Peck. "Mackie's been staying somewhere else since your loan came due. So I did some digging. The showcase was featuring his people so he had to be there." He turned his head to look straight at Peck. "And he was. You just couldn't wait until after the show."

Peck shrugged and undid his suit coat and leaned back, laying an arm over the back of the couch. "After the show when everyone comes outside? We needed to get to him when he was by himself."

"I'm still waiting to hear how a man who owes me more money than either of you has ever seen ended up dead."

"He didn't have the money, that's why he was hiding."

"I'm familiar with the idea, Billy. I've been loaning money for my entire adult life, be useful or you're done."

Billy rushed to tell the story, his eyes slightly widened. "There was a girl. She came out looking for Mackie."

"Girl," Sato sighed, "are you going to get more specific or do I have to explain your place?"

"She was one of the dancers, I think."

Sato knew the look he had on his face. One look at Billy said that the young muscle knew it too.

"That still doesn't explain why you idiots decided to kill my mark."

Peck decided to speak up. "Once she showed up, everything changed. Mackie was struggling with us and that drew her attention." Tilting his head toward Billy, Peck glared at the other man. "Idiot shot at the girl."

"I wanted to scare her, I wasn't going to hit her."

Sato felt a muscle in his jaw flex and the edges of his vision darkened. "You fired a gun as a scare tactic? Within blocks of a Police Station?"

"I wanted to get rid of the girl and finish up with

Mackie, but he must've thought I was going to kill the girl and he stepped in the way."

"And the girl… did she see you? Either of you?"

"It was hard to see. We picked a dark place so we couldn't be seen. It works both ways."

"Well, it doesn't work for me." Sato's deceptively pleasant voice made both men sit up a little more. "Are you sure she didn't see you both? She can't identify you?"

"I doubt it, boss." Billy shook his head and leaned back against the cushions. "Like I said it was dark."

"Doubt and know are two different things." Sato's blood had gone cold, his temper white hot. "You disappoint me, Billy."

The room went silent.

Even the girl behind the desk stopped staring at her phone to look up at him, waiting to see what he was going to do.

It hurt to rein in his anger, but his questions hadn't yet been answered.

"Peck?"

"Billy hit him, drilled him in the back, but it wasn't fatal."

Sato's eyes opened a touch wider. "And is that what you did? Made it fatal?"

Peck shrugged and Sato could feel his blood pressure soar.

"Injured like he was, he'd likely tell the police everything. Didn't think you'd want to have to answer questions from the local 5-0."

Sato gave him a withering look. "Here in Hawaii, the local police are all 5-0."

Peck leaned back and crossed one leg over the other. "Killing him will cost you less in the long run."

"I don't recall making you my business manager, Peck." He stopped Billy from commenting with a look cast in his direction. "While Mr. Peck makes a somewhat irritating yet valid point, you don't have anything that I need now, except your absence."

Billy looked back at him with an open question in his eyes.

"That means, Billy. You're going to leave." He let out a sigh. "Leave this room, my employ, and the islands."

When his words sunk in Billy lurched to his feet, his arm lifting up.

Three hammers clicked back and Billy realized what kind of position he put himself in.

"Should I choose to believe that reaching for your gun is… merely a reflex, Billy. You'll be able to walk out of here with your life."

Billy slowly lowered his hand.

One of the guards walked over and took the gun out of his waistband, while another gave him a pat down.

"You don't get to take your gun with you. I can't trust that you'll dispose of it correctly."

Billy glared up at his boss. "Are we done?"

Sato waited until the guard brought him Billy's gun. He pulled out the magazine and looked at the load.

With a look of disgust, Sato set the two pieces on the desk. "You didn't reload your gun?"

Billy opened his mouth to answer, but Sato waved him off.

"Someone escort Billy to the door."

One of the guards reached out to take hold of Billy's elbow.

"And Billy?"

They all stopped to look at Sato. No one ignored him.

"If you're stupid enough to get caught by the police, keep your mouth shut. If you talk, we've got ways of getting to you… and to people you say you love."

Billy's face went ghost white and his jaw dropped, just a fraction. "I won't say a word. I'm not stupid."

Sato shook his head. "I think you are, Billy, but I think you know what I'd be willing to do if you make this worse. So you take the money I paid you and I want you out of Hawaii by tomorrow morning."

Billy started to walk with the guard and stopped.

"You're really going to let me leave?"

"The last thing I need is a trail of bodies that will lead them right to me. Go before I change my mind, Billy."

The door was almost closed when Sato spoke again.

"Don't disappoint me again, Billy."

CHAPTER 6

They'd managed a few hours of sleep before a detective called them and asked them to come back to the main police office on Beretania Street. Climbing the steep and seemingly endless stairs to the front door had Jackson completely on edge the whole time. Sure, the building was impressive and the seat of the Honolulu Police Department, but the stairs made them really visible and that had the hairs on the back of his neck standing up.

Nudging Hi`ilani up ahead of him, he concentrated on staying right on her heels without stepping on them. It wasn't foolproof but he could try to cover her as much as possible just on principle.

Things weren't fixed between them, not by a longshot, but he needed to do something to keep his nerves in check. On missions he was rock steady. They'd done enough training that it was all second nature.

Protecting the woman he loved more than his own life? There was no preparing the kind of calm he needed.

All he could do was vow to do whatever it took, including putting himself between her and any danger.

Just like Mackie.

His throat felt raw when he drew in a breath.

The detective walked out to meet them at the top step and ushered them right in, allowing Jackson to keep his sidearm in the building. It caused a few curious looks, but when the Chief of D's stopped in to give it his blessing, Jackson finally relaxed, just the littlest bit.

Detective Wong explained as he lead them to his office. "The Chief of Detectives is a military man himself. His father was part of the 442nd unit." He paused for a moment as they preceded him into the office and spoke again when he closed the door behind them. "That doesn't mean he'd let any military man carry a weapon into the department. He did his research. Called an old buddy and checked your record." Detective Wong crossed to his desk and waited for them to sit before he pulled out his chair and sat down behind his desk. "To say he's impressed is pretty impressive on its own. He doesn't just throw that word around. The fact that he wouldn't let me see your record proves that I'm out of my depth with you."

Turning to Hi`ilani, the detective's demeanor changed.

"I'm glad to see you're holding up well, Miss Ahfong."

Jackson's mood dampened a bit. She wasn't okay and the detective knew it too.

"I'm barely holding myself together, but thank you for trying to be kind."

Jackson reached his hand out and she took it with only the slightest hint of hesitation.

"I wanted to let you know that we're trying to locate the man you identified from his mug shot this morning."

"Trying?" She swallowed and darted a glance at Jackson. He tried to give her a smile but it came up wanting. "So you don't know where he is?"

Leaning forward, the detective braced his forearms on the edge of his desk, his tie dangling down against the same surface. "We went to his apartment. It looks like he made a quick exit, left most of his stuff behind."

Jackson shook his head. "Do you know where he'd go now? Family?"

"We've checked with his family. His mother seems genuinely worried." He sat back, smoothing his tie down. "We have feelers out. Sources in his… circle. We'll find him."

"Detective," Jackson hoped he was reading too much into the unspoken, "what are you not telling us? You could have told all of this to Hi`ilani over the phone."

The detective cleared his throat. "We've also heard that people have been asking around about you, Miss Ahfong. Now, we don't have any indication that you're in any real danger. Men like this, criminals like this, don't like to draw too much attention to themselves. They operate best in the shadows."

"But they shot Mackie in public," she shot back, her eyes glittering with tears, "in a park next to a busy theater."

"They kept to the shadows. Concealing their identities." He sighed, shaking his head. "Looking at his sheet I doubt he intended to shoot Mackie. He's a strong-arm for local loan sharks. Intimidation is his thing."

"So you think Mackie owed someone money?"

Jackson turned to look at Hi`ilani, felt her tremor through their physical connection.

"But he's never had money problems." Hi`ilani cringed. "Or maybe that's just what he wanted me to think. He paid for most of that showcase to put us out there for the public to give us a venue." Her head shot up and she turned her tear-filled gaze to Jackson. "This is all because of me."

Jackson wanted to reassure her. "Hey, now… don't go borrowing trouble-"

"What else am I supposed to think? If he had money troubles it was because he was trying to help me with my career."

"He had several performers that he was promoting and representing," Jackson reminded her.

"And if I hadn't interrupted them, maybe they would have just left him alone. Mackie was protecting me when they shot him."

Jackson squeezed her hand, but he had more questions for the detective. "So if they're looking for Hi`ilani, what do we need to know to protect her?"

The detective held up his hands, whether in a bid for patience or quiet, Jackson didn't know, and really he didn't care.

"You have to tell me what you're really thinking here."

Nodding slowly, Detective Wong cleared his throat. "Be careful. Lock your doors. Don't go anywhere alone. Be mindful of the people around you."

Jackson found himself wanting to call the man on his

bullshit. He sounded like a 'stranger danger' PSA on some children's TV station. "I'll stay with her."

He felt Hi`ilani tense beside him, tug on her hand as she shook her head. "No, no. I can't ask you to do that. You're supposed to be helping your friends on their vacation. I know how to watch out for myself. I've got one of those cat things on my keychain. The thing that you can use to poke an attacker. And I'm not planning to go out other than work. So," she put a smile on her face and turned it on Jackson for a moment before she looked away, "you can go show your new friends around and I'll be fine."

"If I go to see them," he told her, rubbing his thumb over the back of her hand, "you can come with me, but I'm going to be watching over you."

The detective was looking between them. "If you'd rather not be alone and aren't… comfortable with Mr. Guard staying with you, I think you said that you have family on-island. They'd be happy to have you home, I'm sure."

She shot up to her feet. "If you say that there are people looking for me, I'm not going to live with my family and put them in danger."

Jackson got to his feet and stood beside her. He wanted to put his arm around her shoulders, but held back. "Then I'll stay with you. I wouldn't want to be anywhere else."

He saw the sadness in her eyes but she nodded. "Okay. Fine. You can stay with me."

She hoped it wasn't just her imagination, the look on his face as he smiled at her.

Love?

Is that what this was?

Had he truly loved her then?

Was this what it was now?

She wanted it to be.

Desperately.

Mackie had been taken from her.

She didn't want to lose someone else she… cared about.

"Can I go home now?"

The detective gestured at the room behind them. "Not unless you want to look through the books again? Take another look at the computer?"

Hi`ilani shook her head. "Not really. The other guy was *haole*. Mainland. He had an edge, but he's not in the pictures. Or maybe it was the shadows on his face, but I can tell you he's not in any of the pictures I saw."

"Okay," the detective shrugged, "then just take care of yourself and we'll let you know if there are any developments."

"Thank you," she told him before she headed for the door. "I don't like being kept in the dark."

It wasn't until they were nearly to the front door that Jackson started to talk.

"Is that what you think?"

She kept her head down, her gaze on what was ahead of them.

"Yes, I didn't tell you why I broke it off with you, but I wasn't trying to keep you in the dark. It was just-"

"Better that way?" She paused at the front glass door, her hand on the bar. "Maybe I'll believe it someday. Are you sure you still want to stay with me?"

When he didn't answer immediately, she turned her head to look at him, and what she saw in his eyes left her breathless.

His hand covered hers where it lay on the bar and she suddenly felt his heat prickle along her skin, traveling up her arm and her lips parted on a gasp as she licked her bottom lip.

"Jack," she bit into the corner of her lip, feeling her heart stutter in hesitation, "if you don't, I'll understand and-"

Looking back on it later she probably would have said she saw it coming, but when Jackson lifted her hand from the release bar on the door, she was gaping up at him in utter confusion.

When he turned her away from the door and pressed her back up against the wall, she felt the air in her lungs leave in a rush.

But when his lips covered hers in a kiss, she'd caught up to his intentions and instead of just taking his kiss, she met him halfway and her hands settled on his chest. She didn't just leave them there either.

Curling her fingers into the cotton of his forest green Henley, she held him tight against her.

When he mumbled against her lips she opened her eyes for a moment and saw him reach out an arm to brace himself against the wall. Belatedly, her mind caught his words from a moment before. Something about not wanting to crush her.

But heaven help her she wanted to be.

He stopped just short of slipping his tongue between her lips, and that brought her mind rushing up to the present.

"Wait. Wait." She panted out the words, trying to even out her heart.

To his credit, Jackson listened to her, pulling back enough to give her a chance to breathe, but not moving far enough away that she couldn't feel the heat of him against her skin.

Or maybe it was a blush that warmed her cheeks.

She certainly was allowed a little blush, especially when she heard some soft laughter coming from the security office just on the other side of the main doors.

"That," she told him, with her heart in her throat, "was unexpected."

He smiled at her, a lazy stretch of his lips. "It was inevitable."

She looked away for a moment and then turned back to look at him. "So sure of yourself?"

His eyes spoke volumes, but hearing the words cut deep into her defenses.

"What just happened between us has nothing to do with me being sure of myself." He stood up, pushing off the wall. "There's always been this connection between us. I was a fool to walk away from you. From us."

She nodded. "No argument there."

He laughed. "I'm glad you're not pulling your punches."

She knew there was a wicked look in her eyes, and she liked the little bit of worry in his gaze. "Then you're going to be ecstatic if you put me through this again." She tried to put as much bravado in her tone as she could, but she knew it fell short of her goals.

Acting was one thing.

But Jackson owned too much of her heart to bluff that well to his face.

When he reached out a hand and cupped the side of her face, she tried to keep her heart in check.

Failing miserably that time.

Jackson held her still and pressed a slow, gentle kiss on her lips.

She grinned up at him when he pulled back.

"I think we should go back to my apartment," she told him and kept her eyes on his even as she felt her cheeks flame with heat. "We need some time to just talk."

"I'd like that." Jackson held out his hand and she took it in hers. "I'd like that a lot."

❦

She knew something was wrong before they'd even turned down the street. Tourists standing at the corner waiting to cross the street weren't looking down at the beach, they were looking up toward the Ala Wai Canal.

Nothing interesting to see up there.

So maybe it was just a feeling inside that said it had to be her.

Fatalistic? Sure! Why not?

Jackson stopped his car at the Police barricade and both of them stepped out of the car. Hi`ilani felt his arm around her and she was grateful for the support as they walked up to the officer manning the barricade.

A quick check of her license and the officer called over the officer in charge to get permission for them to move beyond the barrier.

Stepping down off the curb, his hands momentarily resting on his duty belt, Kyle Ballard made his way to the barricade and after a long look at Jackson, he waved them through.

"Kyle, what's going on?"

He turned to look at her and shook his head. "Someone broke into your apartment."

She could feel the color draining from her face. "When?"

"From what we can piece together from a few people in the area, they broke in sometime in the last two hours." He looked over at the apartment next door to her. "Mrs. Pacheco said it was one man. She saw him leave less than an hour ago."

"Is she okay? She didn't try to stop him, did she?" She turned to Jackson. "Mrs. Pacheco is the sweetest lady, tiny, and at least sixty. If he saw her," her breath seized in her chest and she pressed her hand over her heart and found it pounding in her chest, "is she okay?"

Kyle's face showed some concern as he looked at her. "She's okay. She was just coming back from the laundry machines in the back of the building and saw him through a break in the hedge. When he left, she started to follow him and see if he had a car at the curb, but her laundry basket caught on the hedge and she fell in the gravel." He reached out a steadying hand before she could ask her question. "We sent her to the hospital. She had a few scratches on her arms but her knees took the brunt of her fall."

Hi`ilani shook her head. "I should go and see her."

"No," Kyle reached out and grabbed her arm, "you're not going to go and see her."

"Kyle," she tried to pull away but he held on, "she was injured because of me."

"It's not safe. If they've found you here, they're smart enough to think you'd go and see her. You," he slanted a glance at Jackson, "where have you been since I left you two alone."

Irritation swelled in her throat. "He's been with me, we just came back from talking to Detective Wong. You can't think Jackson would do something like this."

"Well, I'm going to call Detective Wong and check your story."

She narrowed her eyes at Kyle. "Don't you trust me at least?"

"This guy has your head turned so far around, I don't think you can see straight. He shows up out of nowhere and suddenly Mackie's dead and it's likely you were a target too?"

Hi`ilani had a sick feeling in her middle, twisting into her gut. "Jackson isn't involved in this."

Kyle wasn't listening. He'd taken a step to the side and stared straight into Jackson's face. "Well? What do you have to say about it?"

When Jackson didn't immediately answer him, Kyle continued on.

"From what the report says you were there with two

other men from the military who apparently ran off to chase the shooters." Kyle leaned closer and lowered his voice to a cold whisper. "They came back empty handed. Two military men couldn't catch a couple of local thugs?"

"Kyle, stop!" She wasn't just tired, she was getting angry. "They were trying to help. You know Chinatown. There's alleys and recessed doorways. Then you've got the abandoned storefronts. The shooters could have ducked in anywhere to get away. And the two men," she looked at Jackson, "they're visiting from Texas, right?"

He nodded.

"So they wouldn't know what a maze Chinatown can be. At night? With a head start? What you're suggesting is just… it's just-"

"What do you want me to think, Lani?" He almost spit out his words. "I was okay when you broke up with me. I got it. You needed to concentrate on your career. Then less than a month goes by and you're almost killed, and he's around you again?" Kyle's finger jabbed at the air in Jackson's direction. "You can't expect me to ignore it."

"Lower your voice," she pleaded with him, "people are looking at us." She pulled into herself, stepping back from the barrier, her gaze lowering down toward the ground.

"This isn't about us. It isn't even about Jack. When I went out after Mackie, I heard them talking about-"

She stopped short.

Shook her head.

Ground her back teeth together.

"I need to go."

She gasped in a harsh breath.

"I need to get away from-"

She stopped because she didn't know how to finish the statement. Here? Him? The curious eyes of the people on the street? The people looking down from their apartment buildings? Balconies?

Her breaths were short.

Heartbeats erratic.

She was aware that she was starting to sweat.

And yet she felt cold.

Chilly.

Was she shivering?

Turning on her heel she rushed off toward Jackson's Jeep and heard the click unlocking the door. Yanking it open she climbed in and slammed the door shut behind her.

Jackson was only a moment behind her, climbing in behind the driver's seat and closing the door.

She wasn't in the mood for talking and he didn't press. Hi`ilani sat there watching as the crime scene investigators moved in and out of her apartment.

Two men in CRIME SCENE jackets carried out boxes filled with plastic bags, closed up with red tape.

"What do you think would have happened if I'd been there?"

Jackson turned to look at her. She didn't turn to look at him. She was barely holding herself together.

"Don't think about that. Don't think about 'what if.' None of that is going to help."

The men carried out a plastic bag the size of a kitchen garbage bag and she could see that it was filled with her clothes. As the man turned to step down off the curb the bag swung around and she saw that what was in the bag was torn. Or maybe cut.

"They know I saw one of the men."

"Probably." Jackson's tone was guarded.

"But now they're coming after me."

Almost as if on cue, Kyle turned to look at them sitting in the car. His expression was… less than friendly.

"They're not going to let me into my apartment today." Picking up her purse she pulled out her phone and then a browser.

"Are you going to call your dad? I'm sure he'll let you stay there until this is sorted out."

"No." She was surprised at the edge in her own voice. "No. I'm not going to stay there and put them in danger." Leaning up against the passenger side door she looked at him. My tutu lives there with him and my sisters. I can't go there."

"So what are you looking up?"

"A lot of hotels have kama'aina rates."

She was still looking through the search results when the engine turned over and Jackson shifted into reverse. Looking over at him she tried to read his expression. "Where are you going?"

"*We*," he corrected her, "are going to my house."

CHAPTER 7

The guard waved them through the Macomb Gate and he saw Hiʻilani turn to look out the window at the art deco style eagles that adorned the posts on either side.

"I've never gone through this gate before." She leaned forward to look through the windshield. "So this gate is the closest to where you live now?"

"Yeah. I only go through Lyman gate if I need to head in that direction for something." Smiling, he put on his turn signal and leaned forward to look at traffic on the cross street.

He could tell that she was curious, looking around as they drove on. "I don't think I've ever seen this part of the base before."

He cleared his throat. "Probably not. When we were seeing each other I'd take you straight to my apartment and we'd-"

Somehow, she managed to smack her hand over his mouth without actually looking in his direction.

"I don't think you actually need to say it," she told him, her voice a little tight, "no one here to impress."

"You always impressed me." He knew it would sound like a line, but it was true. "You always do."

She lowered her hand and leaned back in her seat. "Well, I'm a little less impressive when I'm on the run."

"Hey," he tried to catch her attention, "you're not on the run. You're being protected."

"On a military base, by a member of Delta Force." She laughed a little. "I guess that's about as good as it gets."

"I'm hoping to make it even better. The guys are on leave along with everyone else in my unit, so it'll just be the two of us."

"Just the two of us?"

He thought he heard a smile in her tone but he had to keep his eyes on the road ahead of them. "That's what I'm looking forward to. I want to make sure that you know I meant what I said."

"Well, a little time together. I have to get back to work on Monday. My keiki hula class that I run for the mall."

Jackson smiled. "That's a few days just you and me."

"As long as you don't get tired of me."

Her last few words were muffled and he chanced a glance at her. She had her gaze turned studiously out the side window at the passing scenery.

"I'm not going to get tired of you, Hi`ilani. That was never the problem."

"You'd be surprised what I came up with. All of the reasons I thought up. Mackie added a few of his own. Kaleo and a few of the others added to the list. All of it came down to that you just didn't want me anymore."

Jackson laid his hand down on the console between them, palm up. "That couldn't be farther from the truth. I know I can't expect you just to take my explanation and then it's all good between us. I'm just hoping to give you a good enough reason to try."

He saw her turn and look down between them. Driving, he couldn't study her expression, but he could feel it when she set her hand over his.

"I'd like to try, Jack. I really do. I'm just not sure what we can do while this whole crazy thing is going on."

Closing his hand around hers he gave it a squeeze and continued to drive, turning onto a residential street in one of the older parts of the base. "We're going to get you through this. And when we do, then I'm really going to do my best to romance you."

She laughed. "Keeping me alive is pretty romantic."

He smiled and let out a relieved sigh. "Good to know."

Turning down into a cul-de-sac he nodded down at the end. "Home sweet home."

It took less than a minute to pull into the driveway and park the car. Lifting their joined hands, he pressed a kiss to the backs of her fingers. "Come on, let me get you inside and we'll figure out what to do from here."

"Sounds like a plan."

He let go of her hand and opened his door, jogging around to the passenger side. When he opened the door, he stood there and offered his hand. She took it, smiling, but watching him carefully as if she wasn't sure what he was about.

To be honest, he didn't either.

So far, everything that had happened between them

since he'd met Truck and Ghost had been improvisation and so far, it was working.

Hi`ilani stepped out on the runner and she looked at him with a question in her eyes. "Umm… you're in the way."

"I am?" He couldn't help but smile at her bewildered expression.

"I thought you wanted me to go inside and see your house."

"I do," he grinned at her, "but there's something I need to do first."

Now she was really confused. "Are we going somewhere? We just got here."

"Oh, we're going somewhere." He gave her hand a tug and she leaned forward with a soft yelp. He let go over her hand near his shoulder and reached down with both hands to grasp her hips and pull her up against him.

She wrapped one arm around his back, the other lifting until she slid her fingers around the back of his neck. The kiss she slanted over his lips was perfect.

And the sound she made when his lips plucked at her bottom lip made him groan deep in his throat.

He turned his head slightly, rubbing his cheek along hers. "We really need to get inside."

She laughed, a full-throated sound that he hadn't heard in quite a while. "Fine. You started this, remember that."

"Oh, I'm trying to remember everything about our time together."

"Why?" Her smile tightened at the corners. "Just in case these guys-"

He closed his mouth over hers, leaning her against the frame of the car as he kissed the idea right out of her. When he pulled back, he liked the dreamy look on her face. "You really need to have a little more faith in me."

Her eyes were misty when she looked back at him. "I'm trying, Jack. I really am."

"All right," he grinned and helped her hop down from the runner. "I want to get you inside so we can relax a little before deciding what to do for dinner. I think you'll enjoy seeing where I live now."

&a.

She didn't get the full effect of what she was seeing until she stood on the front walkway of the house. The walls were painted a mossy green with white wooden trim all over. It looked like it came out of one of those cozy cabin TV shows on cable and she shook her head in disbelief. "When you said *house* you weren't joking."

He chuckled a little beside her. "It's pretty great. When we came back from our first mission the three of us were still living in individual apartments and it was killing us." Jackson touched her back and the two of them walked up toward the front door.

"Some of our neighbors were the new guys on base, enjoying Hawaii for all it was worth. Late nights. Loud music. I almost had to hold Baron back from a fight when some guy started hanging pictures after midnight." He shook his head. "Someone in the housing office called me and said they had an available house. Before I even finished telling Baron the news he was packing his stuff in boxes. Train didn't have much of anything to move so he put half of Baron's stuff in his car and we were moved in in less than a day after we got the keys."

As they stood just outside the door he held up his key ring. "Ready?"

She gave him a thoughtful look. "I'm not so sure now. Three single guys in one house? Are you sure you don't have to run inside and toss out the Sports Illustrated centerfolds you've taped up to the refrigerator or maybe air out the stale beer and pizza smell?"

"Seriously? I think I should be insulted!" He gave her a mock look of indignant shock. "First, we know how to use air fresheners. And second," he raised his eyebrows at her, "no one is going to make us get rid of the centerfold on the fridge. No one. Got it?"

"Hurry up and get us inside," she nudged him with her elbow, "so I can kick your butt in private."

"Big talk," he laughed and unlocked the front door. Twisting the knob, he pushed it open and gestured for her to go first.

Toeing off her shoes, she left them just outside the door and stepped into the entry. She hadn't gone more than a few steps when she stopped dead in the middle of the space.

It pretty much looked like heaven. The furniture looked like it had come from three different apartments but contrary to her prediction there were no bottles or pizza boxes to be found on any surface.

"What do you think?"

She heard his smug tone. And she heard the satisfying

"Oof" when she elbowed him in the stomach. "Okay, fine. I'm impressed."

"It does have one drawback."

She turned to look at him, more curious than ever. "What's that?"

Gesturing toward the other side of room, they walked past the small kitchen and paused in what was a hallway, the only difference from the living room and kitchen area was the wide runner carpet down the length of the house. Straight ahead was a bathroom with a square shower in the corner along with the other usual fixtures.

"Small bathroom?" she shrugged.

"More like only bathroom." He nodded toward the right. "My room." Looking down to the left. "Train and then Baron."

Hi`ilani looked up at him. "I bet Train doesn't hang pictures after midnight."

Jackson laughed. "Not if he wants to live." They stood together for a moment until he gestured to the back of the house. "Want to see the backyard?"

She looked up at him with a mildly suspicious glare. "You have a backyard? Now this I have to see."

Dinner, it turned out, came to them.

They'd had plenty of warning.

The two couples had spent the day on the Ewa side of the island and were enjoying the afternoon at the Dole Plantation Maze and discovering the joy of pineapples in every possible way.

When the knock came at the door, Hi`ilani was still feeling a bit of nerves. Jackson smoothed his hand up and down her arm and pressed a kiss to her cheek before he went to answer it.

He wasn't too surprised when she moved across the floor with him. Whether it was to stand beside him or just use him as a comfort, he was fine. Either way kept her close to him.

Besides, having her close by meant he could see her expression when she saw the couples again.

She was easy enough with the women. Hi`ilani took both of them in her embrace as he'd seen her do with others. Her smile and her gentle energy washed through the room like sunlight after the rain. Hugs and smiles easily passed back and forth between the three, especially when they offered their condolences for her loss.

Ghost was next and Jackson was glad that Rayne stood beside her husband during the greeting.

He saw the other Delta Team leader's surprise when Hi`ilani wrapped her arms around his neck and pressed a kiss to his cheek as she offered him her thanks for trying to catch the gunmen.

It wasn't until Hi`ilani turned to welcome Truck that Jackson really understood what a blessing the Delta Force family was.

The big man treated her like she was made of glass.

And it was probably that sweet gesture that broke through the dam that she had been building since Mackie's death. Crouching down low enough that he could wrap his arms around her slender frame and she could wrap her arms around his neck.

As Truck lifted Hi`ilani off of her feet, she hiccupped a sob into the sudden silence. He held her like that for what could have been a few minutes but no one seemed to notice the time.

Mary, standing at her husband's side, watched them with tears in her eyes and a sympathetic smile on her lips.

When she was finally set back down on her feet, Hi`ilani apologized for the tears she'd left on his shoulders.

"Don't worry," he turned and looked at his shoulder with a shrug, "I've got broad shoulders, I can take a little bit of water."

"This is Hawaii," Mary added, "if you can't take a little water you're in big trouble."

The group moved to the living room area and found their places on the assortment of furniture. The overhead fans helped to stir the air coming in from the screened opening to the lanai.

Ghost and Rayne set the bags of food on the tables. Rayne explained what they'd found. "One of the locals at the Dole center mentioned a southern barbeque restaurant near the base. The way she talked about it made all of us hungry so we picked some up for all of us."

Mary grinned and helped to pass out the paper plates and utensils. "We're so glad we got the chance to actually spend some time with you, Hi`ilani. Your voice is amazing!"

She flushed, her cheeks pinking as she struggled to accept the compliment. "My mother taught me all of her favorite songs when I was a little girl. If anything, it's all her doing. I copy the way she sang and keep her tradition alive."

"I have to admit I had my reservations about the showcase. I thought I knew what hula was," Truck admitted. "They have some pretty silly videos on-line." He shrugged a little, giving him an oddly boyish look. "That's what I get for trying to get trip tips from random YouTube channels."

Mary gave his arm a squeeze. "I love you even when you're silly."

"That's good, 'cause I love you, too. Wife." He grinned as he made his last word fill the room.

Jackson saw Hi`ilani blush and share a look with Rayne.

If he'd worried that the gathering might be awkward as the first time that she'd met any of these people was probably the worst night of her life, he was proven completely wrong.

If anything, they all seemed to rally around each other, sharing little jokes and comments back and forth. The couples asked Hi`ilani questions about the places they'd been and planned to be.

Jackson relaxed in the arm chair and smiled at the group, telling Ghost, "I'm glad you're getting a chance to ask her. She's the real expert on local activities."

Hi`ilani easily brushed that off too. "Except for the beaches," she brought over the napkin holder from the kitchen counter, "living here you'd be surprised how little the locals get to the beach."

Jackson's phone chimed from his pocket and he cringed.

Mary, from her seat beside Hi`ilani on the couch, gave him a look full of curiosity. "Who's that?"

He didn't even have to look to know who it was. That 'tone' was reserved for one person.

Standing up from where he was sitting on the arm of the sofa, he gestured to Hi`ilani that he'd be outside.

The screen door slid open easily enough, He stepped outside and took the call.

"Commander?"

"Hello, Ajax."

He swore he could almost see the commander's expectant expression.

"Sir? Is there something I can help you with?"

The commander cleared his throat and it sounded like he was sitting in his office chair. That thing could squeak like an operatic mouse when given the chance. "You could explain to me why I've been fielding calls from a rather irate HPD officer."

"Not a detective?"

There was a long pause on the other end. "So besides the officer, you're also involved with a detective? I'm assuming that you didn't manage to drag the other Deltas into it. If you had, I'm sure their commander would be in my office trying to rip me a new one."

Jackson looked back into the room and caught Ghost's attention.

"No, sir. The other Deltas are enjoying their vacations. They just stopped in to see us."

"Us, hmm?" The commander's sigh was incredibly eloquent. "So the officer is correct in assuming that you have his witness at your house." It could have been a question. Should have been. But apparently his commander knew him too well.

"Yes, sir. She's here with me. Her apartment was vandalized and the police believe that-"

"Officer Ballard explained his take on the situation."

There seemed to be a bit of humor in the commander's voice.

"Sir, I need to let you know that I'm going to keep her here, at my home. On base. If you have any questions or concerns, I would be more than happy to come to your office or your home and explain my actions."

"Am I also to assume that you're involved with this young lady?"

Jackson looked through the screen and caught Hi`ilani's curious look. He put a smile on and nodded at her. "Yes, sir. I'm as involved as she'll let me be."

"Well, we'll have to talk about this at some point, Ajax. As team leader, your actions are going to change a lot about the dynamics of the group."

Looking at the two Deltas and their wives, Jackson felt confident in telling him, "I believe I've got a handle on this, sir."

An exasperated sigh came through the phone clearly. "Make sure you do, Ajax. If this causes a problem, you'll be the one to answer for it."

"Respectfully, sir. You were the one that asked me to meet with the Deltas."

"Sometimes it's best not to rub your commander's nose in his own orders- requests."

"Sorry, sir. It won't happen again, sir."

"It damn well better not." The older man's laughter had Jackson stifling his own.

Jackson ended the call and stepped back inside.

He certainly didn't miss the way the conversation quieted down when he re-entered the room. "Okay, what did I miss?"

Ghost was the one who answered him. "I think it's time you called in your team."

CHAPTER 8

"Hey."

Jackson set his phone on the coffee table and leaned back against the sofa, opening an arm for Hi`ilani.

Smiling, she walked over and sat on the cushion beside him, tucking her legs under. The casual position helped her look him straight in the eye. "Did you finish with your calls?"

He touched his hand to her back and trailed his fingers up and down her back. She was wearing one of his t-shirts and some pajama pants that Baron's sister had left during her last visit to Hawaii.

It didn't escape his notice that she wasn't wearing her bra under the shirt.

And he felt the familiar weight on his chest that always came with thoughts of her. Of how he'd messed things up.

He was trying to focus on the present. Make sure that how he treated her at that moment was the best that he could. His future depended on it.

"I just talked to Mace. His real name is Whitford

Mason, but don't ever call him Whitford. The only person who can get away with that was his mother and she passed on a few months ago."

He saw the sympathetic frown that touched her lips. "He's working through it. The commander gave him the option of taking leave when he got the news, but he opted to stay. He had his mom's ashes sent here and he put her in a niche at Kaneohe Veteran's Cemetery."

She sighed as he traced the top of his thumb up from the lower curve in her spine to the middle of her back. Leaning sideways she relaxed against his arm. "Where is he now?"

"Well, Mace and Shado are climbing all over Angel Falls in Venezuela. I was lucky to get a hold of them on Mace's satellite phone."

"Venezuela? That's a bit of a distance."

"Well, if there's a rock wall those two are going to climb it. They won't be able to get to a plane for a few days, but I'll keep them informed."

Cradling the back of her head with his hand, he lowered her head as he sat up and pressed a kiss to her forehead.

"Cullen is in Canada with his cousins. The man has Mounties on his mother's side of the family and they're tracking a group of traffickers preying on women from the First Nation. He sends his regrets."

Hi`ilani moved a little closer, tucking her shoulder under his arm so she could lay her head on his shoulder. "He's doing a good thing. I hope they find the people they're tracking. No one should take people away from their families."

He turned slightly and drew her closer, enjoying the warmth of her body with the cool evening air coming through the screened doors. "I bet they'll find them. Cullen isn't someone who leaves things half done."

Jackson felt her lay her palm on his stomach. His tank top was barely a barrier between her hand and his skin. Having her that close was becoming a temptation likely to kill him before he had a chance to protect her.

"You call him Cullen. Is that his nickname?"

Jackson shook his head. "No. Cullen is his first name. Cullen Andrews is the only one of us who doesn't have a name yet."

"I would think it was some kind of requirement for a team as specialized as you are."

He shrugged and turned a little more until his free hand settled on her knee.

Touching her was heaven and torture all at the same time, but he'd never give up the opportunity.

"So far we just call him Cullen. One of the ladies that works at the PX thinks he has that 'vampire' look and blushes every time he goes through her line. He has no idea what she's talking about, but it makes us smile."

She laughed and he enjoyed the sound of her joy like a physical touch against his skin. "You guys should clue him in."

"He could just Google 'Cullen' and 'vampire' and find out himself."

"Maybe," she sighed. "And your housemates?"

"You're going to like them. They'll be back on island probably Monday. Tuesday at the latest. Baron is in Australia swimming with sharks."

She gave a start in his arms and he moved his hand a few inches higher on her leg to give her a reassuring squeeze. "You're joking right?"

Jackson shook his head, chuckling at the sound of her concern. "Don't worry about him. If anyone is in danger, it's the sharks. All Baron has to do is glare at them and they'll roll over and die. He'll catch a flight as soon as he can get to the airport."

Burrowing closer into his side, the hand she had set on his stomach smoothed over his belly and wrapped around his waist. "And Train? That's a strange nickname."

He rubbed his cheek on the top of her head enjoying the silken stroke of her hair against his skin. "What about Ajax? That's what they call me."

"Really?" Her laughter was almost a giggle and he felt her body relax further into him. "I hope it's not because you had to clean the bathrooms during training?"

"Ha ha." He pressed a kiss to the top of her head. "Very funny, but no. It seems that our commander has an unhealthy obsession with Greek wars."

She yawned and sighed. "Ah, the Trojan War. We had to read about it in school. You're the heroic warrior."

He had to pull in a breath to keep himself still as her fingers shifted against his side, driving him near to distraction.

Hi`ilani rubbed her cheek against his shoulder. "I like that."

"You do?"

He wondered if she thought he sounded like he was two years old, but sitting next to her, sharing her warmth, having her touch him and letting him touch her, made all the difference in the world.

Jackson felt like he was getting a new start in his life.

A new chance with her.

He didn't want to push. Not then, not ever. He wanted to give her to chance to set the pace. Jackson was going to wait until she knew what she wanted from him.

Hi`ilani listened as Jackson showed her pictures on his phone of Baron and Train, but she found herself as anxious as she was exhausted.

She just didn't know how to tell him.

So, she picked an easy topic of conversation so she didn't have to go to sleep. Not just yet.

"You still haven't told me why he got that nickname."

Jackson groaned and leaned his head back against the sofa. "If you want to know, I'll tell you, but you've been trying to hide how tired you are. Why don't you get some sleep?"

He took his hand off of her leg and set it on the pillow he'd set up against the arm of the sofa. "I'll be right here if you need me."

Yeah. Exactly what she didn't want to hear.

It would be a little difficult to admit, especially while everything was going to hell around her, but she really wanted him to stay with her in the bedroom.

Not because she wanted him in bed with her…

Okay, not 'just' because she wanted him in bed with her.

Spending time with him. Meeting his new friends. Realizing that the future she'd thought lost to her forever was suddenly possible again.

It was a heady thing.

Hearing that he'd ended things because he thought he was protecting her.

That had thrown her for a loop.

A big fat crazy loop.

All of those tears. All the worry that she just hadn't been enough.

It was a hard truth to hear that it wasn't about any of that.

And she knew that she could tell him that his apology hadn't been enough. She could have thanked him for explaining why she'd gone through all of that, before telling him to walk away.

Finally close that door in her past.

But then all of the feelings started rushing back.

All the excitement she felt every time she saw him. The rush of her heart beating faster just because he touched her hand or said her name.

The heat that curled through her when she felt his lips on hers. When his hands touched her body. When he kissed her… there.

All of that became a possibility again.

And maybe she was ready to give into the feelings she still had for him.

She just had to figure out how to tell him.

"So," she kicked herself mentally for the warble in her voice, "you're going to go to sleep?"

He took a moment to answer and she sat up a little to look at his expression.

Jackson lifted the hand he had on the back of the couch and looked at his watch. "I'm going to check the doors and windows and then I'll keep watch for a while. Catch a few minutes here and there.

"I'll feel better when I've got some backup. I'm sure we'll see Detective Wong at some point and we might see Officer Ballard if he can talk his way through the gate."

She cringed a little and he set his hand on the back of her neck, working his fingers lightly over the muscles in her neck.

"I'm sorry. I shouldn't have mentioned him."

Hi`ilani tried to brush it off. "Kyle's just intense. When I met him, I was telling myself I was over you. And that intense part of him felt good at first." She swallowed and continued speaking even though she felt like she was confessing some deep dark secret to him. "He made me feel wanted. Made me feel… desirable."

Beside her, Jackson shifted uncomfortably. He continued his gentle pressure on her neck, his fingers kneading at the tension. She felt it slowly easing away, but another tension was replacing it… building faster than she thought she could handle.

"Why aren't you two still together?" He bit into his lip for a moment and then released the pressure. She wanted to soothe the angry red line with her kiss. "If you don't mind me asking?"

"I don't mind since I was going to tell you anyway."

She shifted slightly on the couch, moving her weight

off of her knees and leaning slightly in the other direction to get some of the blood flowing into her legs.

There wasn't a problem with blood flowing in other places, not with Jackson so close.

"We stopped seeing each other because Kyle and I went from casual dating and straight to a proposal."

Hi`ilani felt Jackson stiffen beside her. Felt his hand still on the back of her neck.

"Apparently it took him less than a few dates to figure out that I was the one for him. He took me to dinner, saying he wanted me to meet his sister. Which wasn't a huge thing for me. I thought it was going to be fun. A nice dinner, some dancing.

"And when I got to the restaurant it wasn't just his sister. His parents were there, some of his cousins... I'm fairly sure that he might have had some old school friends, which was saying something since he moved here from California a few years ago."

She saw Jackson's smile and narrowed her eyes at him. "What?"

"I pegged him for a surfer."

Hi`ilani rolled her eyes. "You both can act like little boys."

"You didn't accept his proposal."

"No. That didn't go over well. Kyle got pretty angry, thinking I'd made a fool of him, but I never said that I felt like that about him. He knew that things hadn't ended well with us and I'd told him that I wasn't ready for anything serious."

"With anyone?"

She heard Jackson ask the question, but she was a little

distracted by how close he was, the heat of his skin against hers.

"Not right now."

She couldn't tell what his expression meant, but she didn't think she had any clue. Her head was a jumble of thoughts of her own.

She'd been burned by him before.

Burned by his rejection but burned by desire as well.

What she'd felt for Jackson had been love. She knew that and knew that she was still in love with him.

There was no denying the truth to herself.

If losing Mackie had taught her anything, it was that she desperately wanted to feel alive.

And if Jackson was right. The two empty bedrooms would be filled and their time alone… well, it was coming to an end.

Waiting any longer, she might never have a chance.

Just that thought. The possibility that there was nothing Jackson could do to protect her, not if these men, whoever they were, were that determined to find her and silence her.

"Jack?"

She heard his soft groan and it gave her strength.

"I don't want you to sleep out here tonight."

He opened his mouth and closed it just as fast, his eyes moving over her face.

She let a few moments go by before she allowed herself to start to worry.

"Jack?"

He turned toward her and settled his hand on her shoulder, rubbing the pad of his thumb over his soft cotton shirt, tracing the line of her collarbone.

"Whatever you want." He looked up into her eyes. "Anything you want, just ask."

"I need to know," she felt her voice waver and her confidence with it, "what you want too, Jack. If you're just going to do what I want, how is that any different from you making the decision for both of us when we broke up."

She watched as the words settled over him.

Something changed in his expression.

The set of his jaw loosened and his eyes lost some of their shine.

"I thought what I was doing for the best. I had no idea that you'd doubt yourself."

That caught her by surprise. "You didn't?"

"No." He shook his head. "I thought you'd shut the door on me. Toss me out with the trash and count yourself lucky."

The words struck home and stole her breath. "How could you think that?"

He laughed. A short bark of sound that was forced from his throat sounding like it had been rubbed raw. "I wanted you to have what I couldn't have. A future with a man worthy of you. A family to love."

How could she admit that she wanted that for herself, too.

But she wanted it with him.

And really, Jackson had apparently done enough thinking for both of them. Thinking and talking.

Hi`ilani was done with both.

Lifting her hand up between them, she grabbed a hold of the shoulder of his tank top and pulled. Swung her leg over his, straddling his lap.

She didn't sit back.

She didn't try to look at him.

What she needed was to feel.

Rising up on her knees she pressed her lips against his.

She'd caught him by surprise, the gasp she swallowed from his lips was evidence enough.

And she pressed her advantage.

Hands on his chest, pressed between them, she used her position to kiss him, leaning his head back on the top of the sofa.

She fed from his lips, kissing him over and over again as she moved restlessly against him.

It was a heady thing.

Jackson's lips had always been her kryptonite and soon enough she was taking as good as she gave.

His hands were on her waist, then her hips.

When he lifted his head from the back of the sofa his hands pressed her down. Suddenly she pressed tight against the heavy press of his erection.

"Oh," the word burst from her lips as she struggled not to pull away.

She wanted him.

She wanted this.

But feeling the heat and need of his body pressed up against her, fitted against her body, she was in danger of losing sight of her plan.

She moved her mouth to his cheek and then to his ear.

Hearing the sharp intake of his breath when she closed her teeth lightly over the tender lobe of his ear.

He hissed when she bit down a little harder, but she didn't pull away.

No, she rubbed the tip of her tongue over the same skin before she closed her lips over it and rolled it into her mouth.

Jackson muttered a curse under his breath, his fingers digging into the full curve of her hips. "Don't..." he lost his thoughts a moment later when her lips found the tender flesh just under his ear.

When she sat back, she saw him frowning at her, his eyes narrowing on her face.

"Don't stop."

"I don't want to stop." She heard the breathy anticipation in her own voice, but she was sure he heard her. His eyes were fixed on her lips, so even if his ears were rushing with sound like hers were, she was sure he could read her words. "But I want you to take me into your room and-"

He was suddenly on his feet, his hands still anchored on her hips.

She yelped at the sudden change, but also because his hands slid around to the round curves of her backside and pulled her tighter against him.

She wrapped her legs around his middle and let him carry her away.

CHAPTER 9

He set her on her feet and held her close, with just a hint of air between their bodies.

"It's been so long."

She nodded, but her gaze didn't leave his. "Too long," she agreed.

Lifting his hands from her waist he trailed his fingertips up the graceful lengths of her arms, tangling for a moment with the hem of his t-shirt sleeves before carrying on.

And when he'd reached her shoulders, he lifted his hands again to cradle her face in his palms.

"I love you," he told her the truth, his voice shaking ever so slightly. "You'll probably get tired of me saying it, but it's the reason I tried to stay away. And it's also the reason I came to you again."

Her lashes glistened with tears in the softly lit room. The moonlight slanting in through the window gave him just enough light to see the myriad of emotions in her eyes.

He saw love, but he also saw the hurt. Some of it he'd caused. Some of it was the loss of her friend... her mentor.

"I can't fix everything between us, Hi`ilani, but I'm going to stand by you. Even if you stop wanting me in your life, I'll protect you."

She shook her head. It was the tiniest of movements but he felt it because his hands were on her. "You don't need to fix anything, Jack. I loved you before and I never stopped." She drew in a breath and it shook through her body and into his. "I never thought I'd be in trouble like this, but if I had to have someone watching over me, it would be you.

"I've never felt so safe than when I've been in your arms, feeling your heart beating in your chest, breathing you in."

Her words cut him like a knife.

Knowing what he'd taken from her made him all the more determined to give her that and more.

"Hi`ilani-"

"Listen." Her voice was soft, but he heard the plea in her tone and he wanted to listen. Her voice had always called to the deepest part of him.

Deeper than his heart.

All the way into his soul.

She repeated the plea and he listened but he could only hear her.

"The rain," she sighed. "I can hear it on the roof."

So did he.

"And on the leaves."

"Yeah,"

"Do you remember the first time you kissed me?"

Of course he did.

"It was in the rain." He smoothed his thumb over her high cheekbone.

She smiled up at him. "Barely a mist."

He smiled back. "And it looked like tears on your skin."

He could feel her breathing. The gentle movement of her skin against his, just the touch of his hands against her.

He'd used his hands to kill, but what he wanted more than anything else was to use his hands to feel life.

Jackson leaned down and kissed her cheeks before he gave her the barest of kisses against her lips.

When he pulled back, just an inch, she swayed forward, drawn to him.

Just as much as he was to her.

It was a tender moment between them, but the next moment changed everything.

She sighed, a simple exhale.

But he leaned in, breathed it in.

Breathed her in.

And he realized the simple truth.

He needed her like his next breath.

They reached for each other.

Kissed and kissed again as they discarded their clothes between the door and the bed.

It was only when his foot was caught up in the leg of his pants that he fell across the bed, tugging her down with him.

The scent of the rain.

The feel of her supple skin against his hard lines.

Everything rushed in like the current of the ocean, dragging him under her power.

She straddled his body again with a single graceful movement that belied her natural gift of dance.

He rose up on an elbow, snaking his other hand around the nape of her neck. The feeling of her hair sliding over his arm was torture. Between their bodies his dick jumped, pressing against her belly.

A flash of lightning painted their bodies silver, highlighting the pearl of precum beaded on the head of his cock.

Every inch of him heated.

Slanting a kiss against her mouth, he couldn't help but delve within when she parted her lips. Their tongues tangled, danced together.

Tasted.

Stroked.

And he wanted more.

So much more.

Shifting his weight on his elbow, he moved his hand on her neck, wrapping around even more as he tried to think of the best way to pull her under him.

She was faster.

More in control.

Or maybe less. It depended how he wanted to think about it.

If he wanted to think.

And at that moment, all he wanted to do was feel.

Her hand closed around him, wrapped around the

base, stroking up to the tip with one long sweep of motion.

His breath came out as a gasp and she pulled it into her mouth.

Jackson felt consumed.

Felt as if she had swallowed his soul.

Taken it into her own body.

And maybe she had.

Another stroke, down and then up, her palm smoothing over the skin at his tip, nearly cradling him in her palm.

"Are you trying to kill me?"

She laughed and shook her head back, moving her hair about her shoulders like a curtain. The dark lengths framing her breasts for his hungry gaze. When she looked down at him his hand slid down from her neck and his palm traced over her nipple, teasing it into a peak as he copied the touch of her hand on him.

"Kill you? No." She bit down on her lip as he rolled her nipple between his fingers, teasing her flesh. "But I want you inside me, Jack. I need you."

And that was all he needed to take all of his good intentions and cut straight through to the heart of the matter.

"I need to get into my drawer." Looking up and over his shoulder he saw the nightstand open slightly and a couple of foil packets on the top beside the mattress. He turned his gaze back to her face. "How did you-"

"Where else would a guy keep them," she shifted, moving a few inches closer. When she moved again, he shifted with her, higher on the bed.

He saw her eyes darken as their movements together created the most amazing friction between them.

"I would have looked through your wallet," she moaned softly as he wrapped a hand around her to nudge her higher with him, "but I thought that might be a little… too obvious."

His laughter was little more than a soft chuckle deep in his chest.

"Men can be a little dense," he caught her look and continued on, "so feel free to be obvious. I might need the hint."

He took the chance and laid back flat on the bed, reaching his arm back, he managed to pinch one of the packets between the flats of two fingers. Pausing only to open the packet with his teeth, he kept his eyes on her.

Jackson watched her breathe.

Watched the way her body rose and fell with every breath he took.

Saw the way her eyes watched him as if she was memorizing him.

He knew that look.

Knew that he'd created it.

He dropped the packet down on the bed beside him. "Come here," he crooked his finger at her, "closer."

Her smile made him want her even more.

The way she leaned forward, lowering herself down over him, made him shake with desire.

The touch of her breasts against his chest, the way her lashes lowered to hide her gaze…

"I was a fool."

She set one hand over his shoulder, and then the other,

slowly trailing her tongue over her bottom lip. "Yes, you were."

He opened his mouth to speak but felt her roll her hips against him, sliding the heat of her body against him. Root to tip, she turned him inside out, strung him out, sent his heart into overdrive.

Hi`ilani rose up over him, pressed a kiss to his lips, brushed the side of her nose against him.

"You know what else you were?"

Jackson swallowed and let out a breath in a rush of air when she lowered herself down, pressing her breasts against his chest, the stiff peaks making the contact even more frustrating.

"No… no." He pulled a breath into his lungs just so that he could feel her against him again. "What was I?"

She rose up again, moving so that she could look into his eyes. "You were mine."

If he thought he was hard before. Hearing her words. Seeing the sadness in her eyes mixed with hope, feeling her skin moving against his, he ached for her.

He arched his back to slide his cock against the soft curve of her belly.

Her eyes shut and her breath caught in her chest. "Jack, please."

"Please? What do you want? Tell me and it's yours."

"Please," her tone was softer, barely a whisper, "don't leave me again."

It broke him.

His heart stopped short in his chest, his lungs begged for air.

He blamed himself for her fears.

And here she was, letting him back into her life. Letting him touch her. It would be years before he felt like he was worthy of that trust.

Her love.

Pressing his lips up against her, she rose up on her hands on a gasp.

Jackson caught the tip of her breast in his mouth, swept his tongue over the tight bud of her nipple.

Wrapping a hand around her back, he held her gently in place as he pulled her deeper into his mouth, the slightest hint of teeth bowed her back.

Brought a sigh to her lips.

Clenched her thighs around his hips.

She held herself close to him, close enough to cause him pain, but he didn't care.

He welcomed the pain and pulled her closer.

Jackson heard her digging her fingers into the sheets, heard her gasp and pant in time to his tongue, the soft scratch of his teeth.

They moved together, his hips pushing her higher and she urged him on, his name on her lips.

She was off-balance, delirious.

The rain pounding on the roof, the scent of it in the air, the scent of his skin. The scent of the two of them together.

His mouth on her skin.

And oh god, his teeth. His tongue.

Every push of his hips ground him against her. And

she pressed tighter needing to feel his fullness against her skin.

So long.

So, so long.

And she'd never stopped needing him.

She'd tried to move on, but no one made her feel the way he had.

The way he was making her feel.

"Oh Jack…"

His mouth closed over her other breast and the pleasure was so keen it was nearly pain. He was gentle but insistent.

And she pressed down against him and felt the twitch of his erection even while it was trapped between their bodies.

A little shift of her hips and the keen pressure of the base of his cock against her clit sent sparks of pleasure shooting through her body.

"Yes… oh yes."

Jackson. Heaven help her. The things he was doing to her with just his mouth.

More.

She wanted so much more.

Blindly reaching out with her hand she had to fish around a little but there it was.

She felt the scratch of the perforated edge of the wrapper and lifted it off the bed.

"Here, here." She pulled it up and handed it to him. Grumbling when he took his mouth away from her skin. "Can't you do that without- Oh."

She was under him before she realized what he was about.

His arm hooked under her thigh, opening her as he straddled her other leg.

She looked up at him and saw the way his eyes raked over her body.

"You're so damn beautiful."

"You too, Jack." Hi`ilani licked at her lips trying to keep her breathing under control. The last thing she wanted to do was miss a single moment. "So many nights I dreamt of you. Of us. Like this."

He moved closer, heavier on her. The weight wasn't uncomfortable. She liked being under him.

Loved feeling his skin against her.

"Like this?"

His gaze left hers and looked down.

She followed him and saw his hand around the base of his cock, holding it as he leaned forward.

The way he was built, if he had her against the wall all it took was lifting her up and he'd fit snugly against her, but on her back, sinking into the comforter with his weight it was different.

She'd never say a word to anyone, but she liked this better.

Watching his hand, the hard length he held, bared to her gaze. And then the feel of him pressing against her, stretching her around him.

Hi`ilani watched him as he let go, smoothing his hand under her thigh, opening her farther so they could both watch the way he fit inside her.

Stroked her in the most intimate of ways, and filled her.

She lifted her hand and smoothed it up his stomach, smiling at the way her fingers bumped into the ridges of his muscles, the way it made him gasp and tense.

"I love you, Jackson. So much it scares me."

"You terrify me," she heard the truth in his voice. "Touching you, holding you," he touched his hand to her belly and smoothed his thumb over her skin, "making love to you is everything to me. I won't lose you again."

Hi`ilani shook her head, managing to whisper around the tightness in her throat. "I can't lose you either."

"I'm going to hold onto you so tight."

"Then show me, Jack." She grabbed his arms and tried to draw him down to her. "Show me how."

He withdrew almost to the tip and she felt empty, almost scared.

He lifted his eyes to hers and shook his head. "Don't worry. I'm not going anywhere."

And to prove his point he was suddenly filling her again.

And again.

His arm under her leg, holding her close, it felt more like dancing, driving a hard, demanding rhythm and she felt like laughing, crying, everything.

She felt him around her.

In her.

Every breath she took, she took from air that he breathed. The air that had touched his skin.

It never seemed to end, pushing forward, pushing

them higher on the bed, deeper and harder until she was sure she would be able to absorb him through her skin.

The fan above them, spinning through the humid air was all she could hear above the rush of blood coursing through her ears. Spinning and spinning like the thoughts in her head.

She felt light as if she would float if Jackson moved away, she'd never been so grateful for his delicious weight on top of her.

Canting her hips up, his next thrust had her grasping at him, desperate for release. And she was so, so close.

"A little more, Jack. Please. A little harder."

"You are trying to kill me."

She opened her mouth to speak but his hand fell to her hip and he gave her harder and faster.

Hi`ilani took it all and held onto him as if her life depended on it.

A moment later it did.

Her release curled through her body like a wave over the reef, breaking and spinning, energy becoming energy. Pleasure rushed through her veins, traveling through every inch of her body.

She felt him tense against her.

Felt his cock twitch inside her body as her own spasmed around him.

"Jack," she gasped out his name once, twice... who knows how many times.

But she finally quieted down when she felt his lips on her neck, heard his voice murmur against her skin. "I'll never let you go."

It was still dark when she woke up. Most mornings she slept in. Saving her energy for the classes that she taught and then her performances at night. Being up before the sun was not what she did.

Stretching on the bed she turned on her side and saw Jackson sprawled on the bed. He was out like a light and she lifted a hand, stroking her fingertips down his cheek.

He turned and pressed a kiss to her fingers before mumbling in her direction. "Come back to bed, baby."

She smiled and sighed. "I'm still in bed."

"Oh, good."

And he was out like a light again.

Sliding to the edge of the bed, she set her feet on the ground and stood up.

So far so good.

It wasn't that she was trying to get away from him.

No. She just had to use the restroom and really who wants to tell your guy that you have to pee?

Not her. And not the guy that ran super-secret missions to save people.

Besides, she'd be back in bed in a minute or two. What was the harm?

She bent down and picked up Jackson's shirt that she'd worn the night before and slipped it over her head. Darting into the shared bathroom she was very happy that his friends weren't coming back for a little bit. It was going to get very interesting when there were four of them in the house and one bathroom to share.

Closing the door, she crossed to the far side of the room and tried to ignore the slight wince when she sat down. They hadn't stopped at one time the night before. After they'd napped a bit she woke up and wrapped her arms around him, reaching her hand under the blanket and…

She heard Jackson walking outside the door and she felt guilty for leaving the room without telling him. Worrying that he was upset, it only took her a few seconds to finish up and wash her hands.

Wiping her hands on a towel hanging on a rod against the side wall she stepped to the door and opened it up.

"Hey, Jack, I-"

The face that looked back at her wasn't Jack. The eyes were enough for her to see the difference. She was exhausted, but fear lent her strength.

Slamming the door, she screamed.

CHAPTER 10

Jackson leapt out of bed, his sidearm in his hand. It took him less than a heartbeat to cross the room and fling open the door. The man standing in the hall was glaring at him.

Jerking his thumb at the bathroom door, Baron sighed and clenched his teeth together. "I think I scared your girl."

"Woman," Jackson corrected him with a pointed grin.

"Whatever you want to call her, she's going to wake the neighbors and that means-"

"That a one-star general is going to be breathing down our asses."

Baron's smile was almost feral. "Your ass, maybe. I'll throw you under the bus so fast."

Jackson leaned closer to the bathroom door and knocked on it. "It's okay. You can come out."

"Seriously? Is that guy gone? Did you chase him away?"

"It'll take more than you screaming to chase this guy away. He's one of my team."

The door swung open and Hi`ilani moved straight from the bathroom to his side. "I thought you said it would take a day or two."

Baron snorted and Jackson glared at him.

"Why didn't you tell me you were coming in early?"

"I got in on a military transport less than two hours ago. I came straight here. Not my fault this house only has one bathroom." Ignoring his brother-in-arms, he held out his hand to Hi`ilani. "Sorry about that. They call me Baron."

She reached out a hand and shook Baron's hand. "I'm Hi`ilani."

"Oh," Baron gave her a grin, "I know."

Hi`ilani had no idea how rare a smile like that was.

A knock at the front door turned all of their heads.

Jackson pulled her to his side and then turned to put himself between her and the front door.

Before Jackson could ask, Baron held up his hands. "I'll get the door, but I wouldn't worry," he explained as he walked across the room, "the bad guys rarely knock."

Jackson knew Baron was right, but still…

Baron looked through the clear-glass, half-circle window and gestured at Jackson's weapon before he reached the door.

Jackson set his gun down on a shelf built into the wall, tucking it behind a bunch of books. "Hey, guys." Stepping aside, Baron gestured for the men to enter. "Did you get a noise complaint?"

One of the MPs looked back at Baron. "General Sanderson said there was screaming coming from this house."

"That was me, sorry."

Jackson looked down at Hi`ilani and gave her a smile before he addressed the officers. "My girlfriend is staying over for a few days and we didn't expect Lt. Roth to be back from his trip so early."

The attention shifted back to Baron who shrugged. "Consider this a lesson learned. When you share one of these houses, add in another bathroom or two. Sharing sucks."

"It was dark," Hi`ilani explained, moving to Jackson's side, "I opened the door and he was standing there. I'm sorry if I caused trouble."

Jackson noticed that the men were having a little difficulty with keeping their eyes strictly on her face.

Turning slightly, he followed their gazes with his own.

When he looked back at the MPs, Jackson couldn't help but see that Baron knew what he was thinking. Apparently he'd noticed what Hi`ilani was... or wasn't wearing.

"So, is there anything you need from us besides an assurance that we'll keep things quiet?"

He'd caught the two unawares and when they turned to look at him, they nodded and then shook their heads, still a little dazed.

"Thank you, and um... in the future, just keep each other informed about your plans. Okay?"

Jackson hoped that Baron kept his temper in check. He took orders from certain people. Well, two. That was it. Having an MP give them 'advice' pushed on that line. "Thanks. We'll keep that in mind."

The men said their good byes and left leaving the three

of them alone again.

Baron locked the door and flopped down on the sofa putting his feet up on the armrest and one arm behind his head. "So, things have certainly changed while I've been gone."

Hi`ilani looked over at Baron before she met Jackson's eyes. She looked a little shell shocked.

Jackson put his hands on her arms and gave her a gentle squeeze. "You okay?"

Her laughter was a little forced. "Yeah, sorry. I'm just a little tired and now I'm feeling a little silly." She darted a glance around him at his teammate. "I'm sure it wasn't the best first impression."

Looking over his shoulder, Jackson gave Baron a look that clearly told him to behave.

Baron gave him a wide-eyed innocent stare.

Oh, brother.

He turned back to Hi`ilani and leaned forward to press a kiss to her forehead. "Hey, don't be so hard on yourself. You didn't know the jerk was going to show up out of nowhere-"

"To my own house!" Baron sighed loudly.

"Without calling to let us know he was on island."

"And if I had called," Baron cleared his throat, "I can guess what the two of you were doing at that time. I don't think you would have answered."

Jackson felt her reaction. She pulled away slightly, her gaze meeting his with a troubled furrow between her brows.

Her face was flushed red under her tan and he saw the worry in her eyes.

Leaning closer, he touched his forehead to hers and whispered. "Go and finish getting dressed."

"Go and finish…" she looked down at her bare legs and ran for the bedroom.

He watched her go and even when she closed the door to their bedroom he didn't turn around.

"Well, look at you, Ajax. Or should we change it to Odysseus, since she was your once and now future woman?"

Jackson still didn't turn around. "If you're trying to get me to kick your sorry ass-"

"I think maybe I should let your woman know that you seem to be obsessed with my ass."

Jackson heard Baron shifting on the couch and turned. "Kicking it? Sure. That's all of it."

Baron was nodding at him. "And given the look that we got of her ass, I know you've got more than enough to hold onto."

He growled at his friend. "You didn't see her… you didn't see anything of the kind," he informed him, "my shirt isn't that short on her."

An eyebrow crooked up giving Baron a knowing look. "And I have a feeling while I was heading back here to base it was you and not your shirt that was on her."

Jackson glared at him. "Okay, you've had your fun. Stop."

Baron looked back at him with an even stare. "Besides saving her life, you're telling me that this is a thing again?"

"It was always a thing for me. I never wanted to give

her up."

"You were the only one of us who was involved at the time and you were a pain in the ass for months after you broke up with her." Baron yawned and let one foot fall down to the ground, the sound heavier because of his boots. "You know I'll have your back no matter what, but this… between the two of you. You're good? Happy?"

"Everything's been a bit of a rush, but even before the shooting I knew I needed her back in my life."

Groaning, Baron sat up, letting his other foot drop down to the ground. With a hand on the back of the seat, he pushed himself up. "Well, I am going to use the bathroom now that it's empty and then get some shut-eye."

Jackson could only smile at his teammate. "Thanks for coming back early."

Baron looked back at him, his face set in his customarily stoic stare. "Like I said, I've got your back." Shrugging, he added the littlest bit of a smile at the corners. "And by extension, hers too. Go, get in bed and try not to be too loud. Some of us don't have someone gorgeous to snuggle up to."

Jackson kept his mouth shut even though he just couldn't seem to imagine Baron snuggling up to anyone.

One step shy of his doorway, Jackson's second in command added one more thought. "And while she's here, can we keep the amount of feminine paraphernalia in the bathroom to a minimum."

"You're tired, Baron. Go and get some sleep or I'll let Hi`ilani kick your ass. She'd like it too."

Baron nodded agreeably. "And really, the way she looks? I might enjoy it too."

Jackson left his friend standing in the hallway with a one finger salute in his direction. Baron's laughter followed him as he closed the door.

Peck had to turn his body almost sideways to fit through the narrow gate. A heartbeat later he had to crouch down to clear his head through the doorway. Once inside the darkened stairwell he reached up to pluck at the ridiculous cotton shirt he wore.

Sato, the bastard that he was, thought he was something of a wit when he told him to change the way he dressed.

"You stick out like a sore hand, Peck."

"Don't you mean a sore thumb?"

His eyes were hard even though Sato smiled. "You're too damn big to be just a thumb."

So there he was in one of those ubiquitous aloha shirts, but one that was muted in color, moving around the Chinatown area thinking he'd still stick out.

But thanks to the age that he lived in there were so many people on their phones that the only people who seemed to notice him knew better than to make a fuss.

Fear was a helpful thing in his line of work.

The stairs were short, likely made back when the people who lived here when it was a thriving community of immigrants, but amazingly quiet, even under his heavier footsteps.

The upper hallway had all of one working bulb and even that flickered on and off. "What a dump."

The door at the end of the hallway was his aim, at least what he'd been told by the dealer he'd found lurking in the alley outside of O'Malley's bar.

He didn't even bother to knock, just twisted the knob and gave the door a good shove. The lock was old enough that it slipped free and swung open.

On the couch, Billy barely managed to lift his head. "What are you doing here"

"I'm here, because having you hide out isn't helping my boss."

Billy's hand fell from the back of the couch and onto his chest. "He's my boss too."

"Good. Glad you remembered, because he's got a job for you."

Peck moved across the tiny apartment and picked up the ancient coffee pot and took a sniff of the brew in it.

It smelled like sulfur, moved like tar. He couldn't even toss it in the sink, it barely slid an inch down the side of the pot when he turned it over.

"You're a slob, Billy boy. A damn slob." Grabbing the knob on the sink he twisted it. The pipes shuddered and the water found a way out of the spigot, an almost clear gush of water. Good enough to slosh out the sludge. "I'm going to make you some coffee," he turned and saw Billy reaching for the pipe on the table, "touch that and I'll break your hand."

Billy slouched back on the couch cushion. "What do you care? Wouldn't it be easier for Sato if I killed myself?"

"Not at the moment. The boss has a big job for you. A

way to prove that you're not that much of a fuck up."

Lowering his bare feet to the floor, Billy sat up and groaned. He dropped his head into his hands. "What now?"

When Peck set the coffee pot down it made a rather disgusting crunch on whatever crusty remains were on the metal plate.

Once he flicked the switch and saw the red-light blink on, he turned back around and glared at Billy. "We need to get you sober enough to remember the plan."

"And then?"

Peck tugged at the cotton fabric, pulling it away from his sweaty chest. "And then you're going to get yourself caught by the police."

"What the hell? No way! He said I needed to hide out!"

"He changed his mind. With you missing, they're hiding that girl away somewhere. If you were behind bars, they'll loosen up."

Squeezing his eyes shut against the pain of the sunlight hitting his eyes from a crack in the window, Billy cursed. "And you? You're going to be caught too?"

"Idiot," Peck glared at him. "I need to stay out here so I can clean up your mess, Billy. And until that happens… you're more help to us behind bars than sitting here in your own filth."

Hi`ilani barely managed to fall into the chair at the Local Grinds Coffee Shop. "My feet are aching!"

Mary and Rayne took the seats on either side of her,

laughing the whole time. "This is nothing," Rayne leaned in and sighed happily, "it seems like every one of our women has needed to replace their entire wardrobe at some point after meeting one of the men."

Mary nodded thoughtfully. "What is it that the bad guys have against a good woman's wardrobe?"

Laughing, Hi`ilani's attention was drawn to movement across the store. Truck, Ghost, Baron, & Jackson were walking through the automatic sliding doors of the mall.

Together, the three women sighed in admiration.

"Goodness, look at them all together."

Mary reached across the table and gave Rayne's hand a squeeze. "Amen, sister."

Leaning forward onto her forearms, Hi`ilani covered their hands with hers. "They are pretty good looking," her voice completely nonchalant, "not bad, really."

The two Delta wives turned to look at her in unison.

"You're joking, right?" Mary's tone was anything but.

"Seriously?" Rayne's brow furrowed. "Not bad?"

Hi`ilani waited until the men were halfway across the open rotunda and then she leaned in toward the ladies. "Scorching hot and you two know it."

Rayne looked at her and she couldn't help the blush that crawled all over her face and neck.

"Oh my God, you and Ajax? Seriously, and you didn't tell us earlier?"

Mary laughed and leaned even closer. "What did you expect her to do? Until now, the men have been by our sides."

Jackson walked up to the table. "Why do I get the feeling we should all run away from you ladies?"

"I bet the last person you want to run away from is Hi`ilani. Hmm, Ajax?"

Hi`ilani felt Jackson look at her after Mary's little comment and she blushed even more.

Baron was the one who broke into the conversation. "You'd be surprised how thin the walls are in our house. After I got home and we got rid of the MPs, Ajax and his honey didn't get a lot of sleep."

"Hey," Truck grabbed Baron's arm, "not funny."

Shrugging off Truck's hand, Baron held up his own in surrender. "Sorry, sometimes I forget what it's like to be around women."

Jackson gave Baron a good shove. "You mean decent women."

Baron gave them all an unapologetic smile. "Semantics, Ajax. Plain ol' semantics."

"Sometimes," Ghost interjected, "it makes all the difference."

Hi`ilani's phone chimed in her purse and startled, she fished it out. Opening it up she a notification on her phone. "Detective Wong sent me a text. Excuse me." She pushed back her chair and walked over to an empty storefront where there was less noise. Dialing she held the phone to her ear.

A hand touched her shoulder and she turned around to see Jackson standing there, hiding her from any curious eyes. He touched her back with his hand, his thumb stroking her side.

"Miss Ahfong?"

"Yes, Detective Wong. What happened?"

"I'm calling with some developments in the case. One of

the men who shot your friend has been found and he's in our lock up awaiting an arraignment tomorrow morning."

"That's great! Wow, when did that happen? How did you find him?" Her heart was beating a frantic rhythm in her chest. "Never mind, I don't need to know."

"Okay," she heard a happy sigh in his voice, "but if you do want to know you can always ask later. Now, I do have to remind you that we're still looking for the other man he was with and while we have him in custody, he's refusing to talk until he has a lawyer.

"A hold up in the Public Defender's office is taking some time, but we have hope that we'll be able to get information out of him in exchange for some consideration in sentencing."

"That's great, right? He'll give you his friend's name and then I don't have to hide as much."

"What do you mean, as much?" There was a pause. "What's that noise?"

Blowing out a breath she started to answer but Jackson held out his hand.

Hi`ilani put her phone in his hand.

"Detective, this is Jackson Guard."

"What's going on Jackson? Where did you take her?"

"She has four of the best trained Army men on island at her side here at the PX. It's on military property. She's perfectly safe, Detective. And we're on our way back to my house as soon as we end this call."

"Good. I'd still like you to keep her movements to a minimum until we have more information. More people in custody."

"All right, Detective. We'll keep things to a minimum, but I'm not making her a prisoner. So whatever you can do to find that guy's partner, I'd really appreciate it. Until then, I'm going to keep her safe."

"Okay, Mr. Guard. Be sure you do."

Ending the call, Jackson handed it back to her.

Nodding, she tucked it into her purse as she kept her eyes on him. "Thanks."

"No need to thank me. I want you to be happy and you really needed a break." He set a hand on the wall over her shoulder and leaned in closer. "And I'm glad we brought you here."

"You'll be really glad when we get back home," she smiled, "Mary and Rayne helped me pick out some things."

She saw the curiosity in his eyes and felt her cheeks heat up when she saw his eyes change as he realized what she meant.

"Really?"

She nodded. "A few things… that they said won't stay on very long."

He wrapped his free arm around her and pulled her tight against him, bending her head back with his kiss.

She felt his breath inside of her and she groaned deep in her throat. It continued, his head slanting across her lips in the other direction until they heard someone clap and then another person clearing his throat.

Pushing her hand against his chest, Hi`ilani leaned back and sighed. "Do you mind if I kick your friend's butt?"

Jackson gave her another kiss and then leaned forward to whisper in her ear. "I'll hold him down for you."

Hi`ilani smiled when he stood and set his arm down around her shoulders. "I can't wait."

When they were nearly back to the group she looked up at him and spoke with a hint of worry in her tone.

"I was wondering. Tomorrow is Sunday."

"I'm guessing you weren't wondering about that."

"No, sorry." She shook her head. "You told the Detective that I'm not a prisoner."

He nodded slowly, but she saw the guarded look in his eyes. "I did."

"Then," she bit into her lower lip as she considered her words, "I was wondering how you'd feel about taking me to dinner at my family's house."

"Uh-"

She leaned to the side and looked at the rest of the group. "You're all welcome to come."

Mary looked at Rayne before she answered Hi`ilani. "We have reservations at Roy's tomorrow night."

Hi`ilani waved off her concern. "It's one of the best restaurants, enjoy!" She turned to look at Baron and gave him a grudging smile. "What about you?"

He looked at Jackson and they both saw Jackson narrow his gaze at his friend and shake his head.

"Dragging my ass to an airport to run back and help my friend protect his girlfriend? Painful." Baron nodded and gave Hi`ilani a grin that looked completely unnatural on his face. "Getting to watch her family meet the man that broke her heart? Priceless!"

CHAPTER 11

As they drove past the old Crouching Lion Inn, Jackson saw Hi`ilani sit up and look around her seat into the back of the Jeep.

Jackson laughed. "Are you worried he jumped out along the way?"

Shaking her head, she sat back in her seat and sighed. "He doesn't look comfortable back there."

Jackson's laugh almost came out as a cough. "He's slept in worse."

"Really?"

"Absolutely," Baron's voice scratched up through his throat, "we both have, now can you stop talking about me so I can get some rest?"

Jackson swore under his breath and reached into a small compartment in the console and taking out a small Ziploc-like bag he tossed it into the backseat. Hi`ilani covered her mouth to hide her laugh when the bag bounced off of Baron's forehead. "Now put in the earplugs and shut it."

Baron's single-finger salute had both of them laughing.

Turning back to look out the windshield, Hi`ilani sighed and enjoyed the scenery as it rolled by like a long single-take movie shot.

A few moments passed before Jackson chanced a look at her.

"About this dinner," he swallowed audibly, "is someone going to give you trouble about me being there?"

"Me? Why would they give me trouble?"

He gave a half shrug as he kept his eyes on the tightly curving road that moved them past a crowded beach park. "Maybe because you're bringing a *haole* home?"

"Don't you mean two?" She laughed and he found himself smiling, at what, he didn't know yet, but her laugh wasn't tight or nervous, it was genuine.

"What?" He looked down the road and saw some cars slowing to turn into the beach park. "What's so funny?"

"Most people that I know don't a problem with *Haoles* it's just when people start to exhibit behaviors that are a little..."

"Dickish?" He supplied.

She nodded and gave a little, "Hmm. Yeah, I guess you could say that. I was going for superior or entitled, but sure, that works too." Sitting back in her seat she let the wind from outside the window blow across her face. "As long as you don't act like a jerk no one is going to have a problem with you."

It seemed simple enough. "Sure, I can handle that."

"Good. Still, if you change your mind, I can give you money to go to the L & L by the feed store. Tutu's expecting me to help her tonight so I can't just leave or not go." They were already into the heavily shaded part of the road nearing the old petting zoo and coming up on the next beach park. "You're going to turn left at the light across from the baseball diamond."

He gave her a wink. "Don't trust me with street names?"

Hi`ilani let out a loud sigh. "Nothing against streets names or your spelling, but I like to use landmarks for directions." They continued on for a bit before she spoke again. "But, yeah, your reading of Hawaiian words is sometimes... painful."

Jackson slowed to let some beach goers cross at the crosswalk and used the time to turn and look at her. "Well, what do you expect? It's like a foreign language to me."

The last man across the crosswalk gave them a *shaka* in thanks and Jackson put his foot back on the gas.

"Well, it is a foreign language to you. So there's nothing wrong with asking for a little help." She gestured at the upcoming turn lane in the middle of the road and Jackson set his signal as he slipped into the lane.

"So, help me."

She grinned and leaned forward with an arm braced on the dash. "There's three main things to remember about the Hawaiian language. Can you remember three?"

He gave her a look that spoke volumes and she laughed at it, making him groan. "Tell me."

"Number One," she pointed off toward the mountains as soon as they were through the intersection, "until the Missionaries came from the East Coast, the language was purely verbal, so when you read something, remember that's it's phonetic. The missionaries wrote down what they heard."

"Okay. No silent letters. Got it."

She motioned down a street to the right and he set his signal to make the turn.

"Number Two, it's going to seem like you see a lot of the same letters over and over and that's for a good reason. The missionaries started the language with seventeen letters instead of the English twenty-six, and later brought it down to twelve, so that's all we've got."

"Twelve," he repeated, "doable."

"Okay," she gave him a wink. "Turn left on the third street and you can't miss the house."

"What about number three?"

Leaning back in her seat she sighed with a smile. "All that's left are the vowels. A is AH. E is EH. I is EE. O is OH. And U is OO. If you can remember that you can read things out loud and not have people glaring or laughing."

"No silent letters, repetitive, and Ah, Eh, Ee, Oh, Oo." He was nodding slowly as he set the turn signal for the last street. "I think I can hold that in my head."

"Good," she leaned back even further and set her legs up on the dash, her skirt falling back to her mid-thigh, "we'll give it some practice later. I think we still have some of the kids' books around. The girls can take turns listening to you. They'll love that."

He was about to ask about her sisters when he made the turn and looked down at the end of the street. The last house on the end had a big green hedge around the front of the house, leaving gaps open for the walk up to the front door and the driveway up to the covered garage.

As they drew closer, he saw a bunch of people walking along the side of the road and the side streets, all heading in the same direction. A large white tent top rose above the hedge and he noticed a bunch of people helping to erect the structure.

"What's going on over there?" he wondered aloud. "Is there a party going on in your neighborhood?"

Using her hand to steady her on the open window frame, she looked up and shook her head. "No, that's just the tent."

"Just the tent?" He shook his head. "It looks like the tent we set up during the last training for a command post. I thought you said this was just a family dinner?"

Her head rolled slightly to the side to look at him with a smug grin and a little glitter in her eyes. "It is a family dinner. Half the neighborhood is related to us and the rest are *kalabash*, like family. Can't leave folks out. So, one Sunday a month, *Tutu Leo* makes Sunday Dinner for the family and we all come over."

"I'm afraid to ask how many people that means." He felt something scratch at the back of his throat.

"'Then don't ask." She raised her hand to wave at someone walking on the side of the road. "Hey!"

They called back and then Hi`ilani settled back into her seat. "Go ahead and park along the left side of the street. Everyone's fine with people parking there when they have to bring their cars."

A little eager to get inside and maybe eager to try to get this over with, Jackson turned a U in the wide street and parked along a chain-link fence covered in some kind of clinging vine.

Getting out of the Jeep, he stretched his legs a bit, waiting for her to join him, but when she didn't walk around the car, he found himself moving around to her side. He found her, crouched over the vine, her hand cupped around a ball of white flowers.

She must have seen him from the corner of her eyes and waved him closer.

He stepped closer and stood at her side for a moment before she tugged on his jeans. When he crouched down beside her, she moved back from the flowers and waved him closer. "Smell this."

If it had been one of the men from his unit he would have thought twice. The things that they'd made each other smell over the last year... well, it wasn't good. Not anywhere near good. But, as he leaned over the flowers in her hand, he drew in a slow breath.

"That's really nice."

She beamed up at him and straightened her legs so that for a moment she was taller than him. "That's *pikake*, a king of jasmine flower. It's spelled P-I-K-A-K-E."

He straightened up, trying not to stare a little too long at her hips and her breasts on the way up. "P-ee-K-ah-K-eh?" He sounded out the word that she'd just spelled for him.

"Yes!" She jumped a little in the air, but she still couldn't quite look him in the eyes. "That was great. Once I tell the girls-"

"Let me guess," he sighed, "they're going to spell everything for me?"

"Well, at least the things they know how to spell. Don't be too afraid." She walked up to the house and looked into the window of the backseat. "What about Baron?"

Jackson opened the front door and lowered the backseat windows. Taking out his phone he typed in a quick message and sent it.

Hi`ilani heard the phone beep from inside the car.

"I let him know where to find us. When he wakes up, he can join us."

She gave him a curious look and then shrugged continuing on toward the house.

"Wait." He called after her and started to jog to catch up. "Why should I be afraid?"

She walked along beside him, waving at a few of the people heading in the same direction.

They didn't even make it up to the front door before the screened door swung open, banging against the side of the house. Two girls dressed in jeans shorts and tank tops came running down the walk barefoot with their hair swinging behind them in two long braids. "Brace yourself," was all she said before the two jumped and hugged her at nearly the same time.

As a surprise attack, it was well planned and he had to give the girls credit for the coordinated assault. The taller girl got her arms around Hi`ilani's neck and the shorter, probably younger girl, latched her arms around her older sister's waist and hugged tight enough to earn a loud exhale.

If he hadn't been quick enough to brace a hand on the middle of her back, the whole group would have ended up in the grass on the small front lawn.

"Hey, hey!" Hi`ilani was laughing too hard to say much

more, but her smile was telling. She was enjoying every second with the little girls.

And when the door swung open again he had barely a chance to look up before he saw a rubber slipper flying through the air.

It sailed right over the girls and landed with a dull thump on the ground. All three girls went silent and turned their heads to the doorway. The woman standing in the doorway had eyes that promised mayhem, but given the soft lines of her face and Hi`ilani's deep affection for her, he knew it had to be mostly guff. Her hair was a pile of grey curls above her over-sized t-shirt with its neck cut out in a wide curve. "Look at you three. Makin' so much noise I had to come out in my *boroboro* shirt."

She looked him over from head to toe and one of her eyebrows seemed to arch higher as she continued all the way down to his feet.

"*Aiyah*, Hi`ilani, why you no call and tell me you bringing one handsome *buggah* to *dinnah?*" She sighed. "*Nevah mind.* Come inside. And you two," she pointed at the younger girls, "you show him out back. Make sure he get something to drink, then come back inside *fo' help.*"

Before he could say anything, Hi`ilani gave him a little wave and followed the woman inside and the two girls latched onto his arms and led him toward the garage. They walked through an opening at the back of the wall and on through to what looked to be the back yard. The grass was greener around the edges of the yard, but given the placement of the tent in the center of the space, he figured that it went up often enough that the dirt under the tent was showing and just the heartiest of weeds had managed to poke through and remain alive.

Behind the hedges, the yard was teeming with plants of all different sizes, shapes, and colors. He knew if he got the chance to ask her, Hi`ilani would likely know all of the names.

Jackson couldn't help the smile he felt on his lips at the thought of how beautiful she looked while she was inhaling the scent of that pikake flower she'd shown him. How he'd ever managed to go without her for the last year... he should have his head examined. When the girls ushered him toward the tent, one of the girls shouted for her father and he didn't expect that the answer would be so immediate.

"What you girls need?"

"We need to show you something." That was from the little girl. He knew that Hi`ilani had told him their names before but he was a little overwhelmed at the moment and just as soon as he sat down, he was going to ask them.

"Come around," he called out. "Inside the tent. *Tutu* going *bus' me up* if I *no get* the tent set up in time."

Given how much the girls were laughing, Jackson knew he was going to have to ask Hi`ilani what that phrase meant. It certainly didn't sound pleasant.

The girls were content to drag him along, even when he thought he should probably find Hi`ilani and stay by her side, but once the girls had a mind to do something, they could certainly do it. Turning the corner at the end of the tent they marched him right up to a man who was lifting and opening chairs like he'd been doing it for years... he probably had.

"Papa?"

"Eh," he barely lifted his attention from the chairs that he was setting up alongside the row of wooden banquet tables, "*wassup?*"

"Papa, this is Hi`i's boyfriend." The little girl had sing-songed the whole sentence in a tone that sounded like she was tattling on her sister, and then again, maybe she was.

It still didn't prevent him from starting to sweat.

The man before him wasn't big. He wasn't built of any muscle that he could see, but when he raised his gaze to look him straight in the eye, he didn't have a smile on his face like Hi`ilani's grandmother, her *Tutu*. No, this man looked at him the way a man might look at a car or a horse, assessing his worth in a few precious moments.

Her father finished his assessment with a little, "Huh," and a nod, but that didn't mean much. He did cast his gaze around the tent and then end up back square on Jackson's shoulders. "So, you *gon'* stand there? Or you *gon'* help?"

The girls let him go, like turning a pig out to slaughter, then joining hands they skipped out of the tent to god-only-knows-where, leaving him alone with their father. He nodded. "Oh, I'm definitely going to help, but I should probably introduce myself." Stepping forward, he held out his hand. "I'm Jackson Guard. I know Hi`ilani from-"

"When you *wen'* break her heart." His father looked at his hand and then moved to pick up a chair and opening it to set beside the table. "I know you."

Jackson nodded, knowing full well that he deserved the dig. "I've apologized to her, sir, and she's accepted my apology."

A huff was next and so Jackson picked up a chair from

the stack leaning against the house and set it down at the end of the long table.

They worked together in silence for a bit and when Jackson had finished one long row he looked up and saw that Hi`ilani's father had already finished a full table.

Turning to pick up the next chair he came up short. Another inch or two and he might have knocked her father down into the grass and dirt under the tent.

Charles Ahfong was a small man but it was not a reflection of his character. He exuded a solid, straightforward confidence that made Jackson stand a little straighter. Hi`ilani was proud of her father's past as a paniolo, a Hawaiian cowboy, and how he'd worked hard day and night to give his daughters the best education that he could afford.

When Charles looked up into his eyes, Jackson felt himself under the microscope.

"You made my baby cry fo' days." Instead of anger, there was sadness in his tone. "I said I'd hogtie you and let her drag you behind one horse." His tone hadn't changed, but the smile on his lips said Charles was considering the pain that it might cause him. And that he was enjoying the idea a little too much. "But she no like hurt you."

"Even though I deserved it."

"No argument *hea*." Charles folded his arms across his chest. "*Jus'* tell me you *goin' do bettah* this time."

"Yes, sir."

A noise behind him turned his head and Jackson stared at the corner of the garage as two of the biggest men he'd ever seen stepped out into the sunlight.

The smaller of the two, and that was a negligible

distinction as both must be the size of full grown grizzly bears, gave Jackson a look that spoke volumes.

Volumes on torture.

"*Wassup*, Uncle Charlie?"

Charlie smiled at the two and nodded at them. "Hi`i brought Army Boy."

By the looks that the men gave him, Jackson knew that they'd heard about him.

He wondered if he might be the one in need of a bodyguard.

The two just stood there as if they were sizing him up to see how big of a hole they'd have to dig.

"Hey," Hi`ilani paused at the top of the steps down from the porch, "how are things going out here?"

The two mountains of muscle rushed past Jackson with amazing speed. One took the platter from her hands and the other picked her up off of the porch and carried her against his chest like a toddler.

By the burst of laughter from her lips, Jackson knew she was having a great time.

"Junior, put me down!"

"Not yet, cuz!"

When his brother reached for her, Junior shook his head and tucked her under his arm like a football and rushed away with his bother chasing after them.

Charlie called after them. "You boys no be stupid, yah?"

When Junior finally slowed down at the end of the yard, both men were belly laughing, showing no lack of breath even with the wild run across the yard. "They play a lot of football?"

Charlie crooked a brow at Jackson. "Junior *wen'* to BYU and Wes *was one* Warrior at UH."

Well, that figured.

"You boys bring her back before Tutu *go aftah you wit' her slippah!*"

That only started them up again with Wes tossing Hi`ilani over his shoulder. She bounced around against his back, her hands trying to find something to hold onto, but the tank top that he was wearing wasn't tight enough to give her any purchase.

The side gate opened and more people descended into the yard. Instead of it stopping the crazy, it only added more people into the mix. And if Jackson had thought that Junior and Wes were huge, the last two men through the gate looked more like stunt-doubles for Dwayne Johnson.

Hi`ilani's father nudged him with an elbow. "You better go get her."

Almost as if she heard the softly spoken suggestion, Hi`ilani looked up, bracing her hand on the back of her cousin that had her tossed over his shoulder and gave him a laughing wave.

And then she crooked her finger at him.

Oh, the game was on.

A few minutes and a couple of bruising blows later, Jackson had Hi`ilani riding piggy back as he dashed for the tent.

Reaching the relative safety of the shade, Hi`ilani raised her arms in victory and her cousins who would easily form a winning defensive line in the NFL were cheering and whistling in celebration right along with them.

Tutu Leo stepped outside and stopped at the edge of the porch, her hands on her hips and murder in her eyes. "Wash your hands! *Almos' time fo' eat!*"

The cousins marched off past the couple, a few of them smacking Jackson on his back as they walked by.

Junior was the last man to step around the corner, only to pop his head back into view. "Army boy, you brought *one noddah haole wit'* you?"

Jackson nodded and laughed when Baron stepped into view, pointing after the men. "Those are her cousins, Baron."

"Cousins?" Baron shook his head as if he needed to clear it. "I thought the mountains were moving."

Hi`ilani rose up on her toes and gave Jackson a kiss on his cheek. "You two better grab a seat before the boys come back."

Waving at Baron, she ran up into the house to help with the food.

"Boys?" Baron stepped up beside Jackson. "Does she need glasses?"

Hi'ilani sat beside Jackson on the grass in the cool evening air, her head on his shoulder as her sisters danced in front of the tent. Junior had his ukulele and Wes his guitar, but what really had her smiling was her Tutu Leo singing along.

"Hey."

She looked down and saw Jackson's hand covering hers in the grass. Looking up she met his gaze. "Hey."

"Your grandmother is pretty amazing."

"Yeah, she is." She couldn't help the broad grin that stretched across her lips. "After my mom passed away she was always here for us. Taught me how to cook. Taught me how to smile when I wanted to cry. She's the best kind of people."

Jackson leaned in and pressed a kiss to her lips. "Of course she is… you couldn't come from anyone else."

"Jack," she felt tears gathering in her eyes, "that's so sweet. I-"

A heavy thump beside her turned both of their heads.

Baron was sprawled out in the grass staring up at the stars. "I'm full."

Before Jackson could speak, Baron turned his head. "You can keep your thoughts to yourself, Ajax." With a sigh, he turned his head back to look at the dark canopy of the sky. "Seriously, this is as close to heaven as it can get."

Hi`ilani heard Jackson laugh softly before he leaned in against her shoulder. "He's drunk."

"Drunk, yes." Apparently Baron had excellent hearing. "But I think I'm getting to appreciate this living in Hawaii thing." He lifted a hand and made lazy circles in the air. "Those cousins of yours," he rolled his head to look at Hi`ilani and then the wince in his expression said he regretted the sudden motion, "they're okay guys. Scary like crazy, especially the looks they were giving Ajax earlier, but I think you're beginning to grow on them, man." Baron chuckled. "Not that they need to get any bigger." He groaned a moment later. "Just FYI, brother, I may or may not have told one of them you were looking to learn sumo wrestling from them."

Hi`ilani felt Jackson lean against her shoulder and she giggled when she felt his breath against her neck.

"Save me, baby."

She touched his thigh and licked her lips. "You'll owe me."

He pressed a light kiss on the shell of her ear. "I'll make you scream my-"

"Hi`i..." Kailani, her nine year old sister barely beat their youngest sister, Leilani by a foot. "Tutu says it's your turn. Everyone's waiting to hear you sing."

"And dance," Leilani added for good measure.

"Hui!"

All heads turned to see Tutu Leo at the front of the gathering. Hi`ilani knew without a word what song her grandmother wanted her to perform. The mu`umu`u that she wore was a special one. One that her mother had sewn for her mother, long and graceful with sleeves that reached almost to her wrists, leaving her golden Hawaiian bracelet visible in the lights. The dark blue velvet facing along the neck gave the gown a purely elegant feel.

Hi`ilani felt tears prickling in her eyes.

"All right you little monsters. Go and get your ukuleles to play and then after this it's *moemoe* time for both of you, tomorrow is school."

The little girls rolled their eyes at their sister, but she knew it was all love. They liked to grouse and groan, but they knew they had an audience.

The two rushed off and Hi`ilani leaned closer to Jackson and pressed a quick kiss to his lips. "I hope you'll like it."

Jackson watched as Hi`ilani and her sisters joined their grandmother at the front of the group.

The two little girls picked up their ukuleles and quickly made sure they were still tuned while Hi`ilani embraced her grandmother and then with her hands on her grandmother's arms, they both leaned in to touch their noses together and rested their foreheads together for just a second.

"What's with that?"

Jackson looked at his friend who was now braced up on one elbow, his hand against the side of his face. "The kiss?"

"Kiss?'

Baron sat up even more and looked back at Jackson. "I know I've had a few, but there was no kiss just now."

Laughing under his breath, Jackson shook his head.

"*Honi*," he explained, "it's a Polynesian kiss, kind of like how the French do that 'air kiss' when they get together. *Honi* is different in that it's not the nose touching that makes it a really intimate thing. They're sharing their breath with each other."

It took a moment before he saw Baron moved and even then, it was a slow up and down nod. "You certainly know a lot."

Jackson shrugged. "You spend enough time with locals and you kind of pick it up."

"Uh huh." Baron's laughter was a little sharp and Jackson didn't have to look to see that his friend was watching him with open curiosity. "So, have you practiced this custom?" When Jackson didn't immediately speak, Baron continued. "Or are you going to tell me that you don't *honi* and talk."

Jackson might have shoved Baron back down into the grass, but he didn't get a chance to. The three Ahfong daughters were up in front of the group with their grand-mother standing next to Hi`ilani.

Even in casual clothes she looked radiant.

Performing certainly was what she was born to do.

When a few of her cousins made a fuss with their

shouts and whistles she shook her head and held out her hands. *"Kuli kuli,"* she told them and the men responded, quieting down. "My Tutu asked me to perform a song that means a lot to our family and so for our last song tonight, we're going to perform 'I'll Weave a Lei of Stars for You.' It was the second song that my parents danced to at their wedding after the Hawaiian Wedding song, and when we think of our mother," Jackson watched her eyes tear up and saw the way she bit into her lower lip to steady her nerves, "this is the song we sing, knowing that she can hear us in heaven."

Just to add her stamp of approval on the edict, sweeping a look around the assembled group. *"No make A-, yeah?"*

The group was quiet and the mood in the yard took on a more somber turn as Hi`ilani took her place a few paces away from her grandmother. Behind them, one of the girls counted in a stage whisper. "One, two, three, four." And both of them started on the same downstroke across the strings.

After a few measures of the background music Hi`ilani and her grandmother began to dance.

Beside him, Baron breathed out a soft huff of breath. "Never seen a grandmother so graceful."

"Be nice, Baron."

"I am," his friend sounded offended. "I'm serious. Okay?"

Jackson nodded. "Okay."

They watched together as the four performed and Hi`ilani's pure voice reached right into his chest and grabbed a tighter hold on his heart. The lyrics in the song spoke of love and longing. Sentimental memories and hope.

People talk about hula as telling a story with their hands but it's so much more than that. When a performer really puts their heart and soul into it, it almost feels like the words come alive in their bodies and the expression on their faces, and in their eyes.

When the song was over Jackson and Baron cheered along with everyone else, but Jackson felt like he'd come a little closer to Hi`ilani in that moment. He'd seen and felt her love for her mother, heard the longing for their loss, and heard the honor they did for her memory.

If there was a way to fall more in love with her, it had just happened, and he was more determined than ever to get this whole thing over with so they could concentrate on the future.

He needed her safe.

Soon.

When they got back to the base, Baron was just conscious enough for Jackson to hold him up long enough to dump him on his bed.

Closing the bedroom door, he shook his head. "Sorry about the snoring. He doesn't do that when he's not-"

"Drunk off his ass?" She waved it off. "I get it. Looks like soldiers party almost as hard as musicians."

He gave her a look but she waved it off with a laugh. "Not me. You know that."

"You didn't even have a drink tonight."

She shook her head. "I could have but I still don't like

to drink in front of the girls." Hi`ilani yawned and looked up at him. "Thanks for coming."

He shook his head. "It was really nice. I don't think I'll ever see you perform and not feel like my whole world is changing right in front of me."

"You say the sweetest things, Jack."

"I mean every word, Hi`i. When you perform you show the world your soul. And even though I already think you're the most beautiful woman in the world, when I see your light up as you perform, you're breathtaking."

They stood there, watching each other.

And he was aware that her breathing had changed. A little faster, a little deeper.

Her eyes had changed. Darker and then darker still as he looked he saw in her eyes nearly brought him to his knees.

How he'd lasted so long without her, he just didn't know.

"Hope."

The corners of her mouth turned up a little. "What's that?"

Until she asked the question he hadn't known that he'd spoken aloud. "I was asking myself how I managed being away from you. I kept my mind focused on training. On missions. Building a connection with the other Deltas. It was my job to keep them alive and that's how I kept my focus.

"But when it was at night and I was alone with my thoughts. You were always there."

"Jack…" she touched the side of his face with her

fingertips and it felt like electricity tracing over his skin.

"What kept me ready and alive was the thought that someday down the line I might get a chance to make things up to you. And the hope that you'd forgive me. Hope."

He let the words fall between them, waiting to see what she might say.

Jackson held out his hand and readied himself to wait. He'd just said a lot more than he'd intended to say and wasn't sure how she'd take it.

She took his hand and smiled at him with her eyes soft and glistening with loving tears.

"Come on, Jack. Let's go to bed."

CHAPTER 13

Morning rolled around and Hi`ilani had never loved a Monday so much. She woke up to Jackson's mouth on her neck, his hand smoothing over her hip and down her thigh. Half-awake she rolled onto her back, opening her thighs as she saw colors of dawn painting the ceiling with a wide-diffuse wash of light.

She wrapped her arms around his neck and his hand trailed up the inside of her thigh. Just as his fingertip began to trace her slick folds, her hips bucked up and Jackson's finger slipped deep inside of her.

He groaned in her ear and she clung tighter to him.

"Jack-"

He covered her mouth with his for a moment and when he drew back he smiled at her. "Train showed up this morning. We've got a full house."

She was struggling to follow his words as he slid his finger out and when he slid back in, there were two.

"So, we're going to have to be quiet."

Hi`ilani's fingers dug into his shoulders as his fingers

continued to slide in and out of her body. She blinked, trying to clear her head, but it didn't seem to matter. Everything was focused on the feeling of his fingers and the weight of him against her leg.

"Can you do that, baby?" He bit his lip and she licked her own wanting to taste him. "Can you keep quiet?"

The look in her eyes flared with challenge. "I would think you'd want me to scream. Don't you want your friends to know?"

She knew he wasn't like that. What they had between them had always been that.

But still, she liked to wave the red flag in front of him, because Jackson always loved a challenge.

He sat back on his knees, withdrawing his fingers entirely from her.

She knew he could read her expression, she wasn't making any pretense. Hi`ilani had no problem communicating her displeasure with him taking his hand away.

Shaking his head at her, he moved over to the side of the bed to grab a condom out of the nightstand, he pushed himself back up onto his knees.

Hi`ilani glared at him and shook her head. "Don't bother opening that."

He held up the packet and smiled down at her. "This?"

She folded her arms over her chest and she saw his eyes lower to look at her. Folding her arms had lifted the hem of the shirt that she was sleeping in.

Hi`ilani knew what he was looking at. The fan circling high above their heads was enough to rush cool air over her and her skin tingled with the chill where his fingers had spread her slick heat on her skin.

Heat. That was in his gaze when his eyes met hers again.

Oh he wanted her just as much as she wanted him, but she was going to make him work for it.

Raising the packet to his mouth, he opened it in one long pull.

Her eyes followed his hands as he pulled the condom from the wrapper and her fingers itched to snatch it from him and roll it down over his length.

When the temptation became almost too much, she pressed both hands flat against her belly. The touch shook her. And images rose up in her head. A baby, swelling under her hands.

The flash of a gold band on his left hand.

And yes, oh yes, his hard cock bare and inside of her.

He said something, but she'd missed it while her head had been elsewhere.

"Hmm?"

His grin was knowing. His eyes glinting with mischief.

And before she could understand what he was about he moved to the side and turned her over on the bed.

Pushing up on her hand, she turned to look at him and what she saw turned the anger welling up inside of her to desire.

He moved behind her, nudging her feet apart with his knees.

Jackson set his hands on her hips and pulled her closer until her sex was pressed tight against his thickness.

A gasp passed from her lips.

Her head dropped down as she struggled to catch her breath.

She felt his hands smooth over her backside, molding to her body, leaving tingling heat in their wake.

Pressing back against him, she felt his fingers dig into the fullness of her and the deep curl of his hips as he slid his cock along her heat.

Jackson sucked in a breath and pressed against her tighter. "Tell me," his words were a demand, but she could hear a plea in his tone, "tell me you want this. That you want me inside you."

"Yes." She didn't hesitate. Didn't play. She wanted him and didn't want to wait a moment longer. "I want you, Jack. Now."

§

Something inside of him broke. That last layer of protection around his heart disintegrated as she lowered herself down, pillowing her head on her arms.

She was in his hands, her body open to his, her need plain for him to see… the scent of her made him rock hard.

He needed her. More than just sex or the heady rush of an orgasm.

He needed her in his life, his bed, and mostly his heart.

And he wanted to give her the world.

And children.

The thought staggered him, twisted something deep inside him at the thought of her rocking their babies to sleep, the sight of her feeding them from her breast.

Hi`ilani had become everything to him. Friend, lover, and hopefully soon, wife and later a mother.

"Jack?" She rocked back against him and her voice had the edge of a sob. "Jack, please. I need-"

He had his hand on her lower back, his palm flattened over the long graceful line of her spine, and his other hand wrapped around the base of his cock.

It took the space of a heartbeat to notch the tip of his cock between her folds, and then with a heavy indrawn breath he pulled himself up and thrust deep inside of her.

Later he might remember that he'd groaned loud enough to wake the dead, but at the moment he had no idea. He saw stars, pinpricks of light at the edges of his vision as she enveloped him tightly inside of her.

"So tight," he panted and wrapped his hands around the curve of her hips to hold her steady as he thrust into her again.

Every stroke pulled and tugged at him.

The only sounds that he could hear beyond the rush of blood through his ears was the gasping breaths from her lips and the slick slap of sounds as he bottomed out again and again.

"More."

She'd whispered the words, but it replayed again in his head like a siren.

He finished his next thrust and bent over her, pressing his chest to her back until he was able to nip his teeth at her shoulder.

She moved restlessly under him and he loved the way she looked with her lips parted and her body pressing back against him.

"You want more?"

"Don't play, Jack. You know I do."

"I'm not playing. I'm going to love you more, just hold on."

He pushed up from the mattress with one hand and the other swept over her sweat slick back.

Jackson saw the dawning realization in her eyes as he wrapped his fingers around the thick fall of her hair. She smiled a second before he leaned back and tugged.

Hi`ilani rose up on her hands with a throaty laugh and her back bowed as he kept a tight hold on her hair.

"You're going to like this," he promised her with the rough scratch of his voice. "If you want me to stop-"

"I want," she squeezed tightly around him and released her own breath in a sigh, "I want it all."

And then the time for talking was over.

He felt her open her knees a hint wider, felt the tight hug of her body on his erection, and as he drove her to the brink of her orgasm and then far, far over the precipice, he found himself tumbling right along with her.

He was almost asleep beside her when someone knocked on the door.

Pushing himself up on an elbow he glared at the wooden door as if it might make the person go away. "What?"

The not-so-whispery-whispers that made it through the door said that both of his housemates were outside. "Sorry to… interrupt your rest, but Hi`ilani has a couple of messages on her phone. One of them from HPD and-"

Jackson opened the door wide enough to look out

without the two seeing that he was naked or catching a glimpse of the room at all. "Thanks, Train."

He took the phone from his friend's hand and saw the knowing smile on the other man's face. "I don't get to come inside and see her with my own eyes?"

He heard Hi'ilani's furious gasp from her place behind him.

"Don't you dare-"

"We'll be out in a few minutes after she checks her messages, okay?"

Train shrugged at the question and gave his friend a wink too. "No rush," he laughed, "we'll wait."

He shut the door and set the lock even though it wouldn't actually be a deterrent if one of the men had to get into the room. All of them were perfectly capable of getting through almost any door, but only a few of them liked doing it with tools. Most of them just leveled a door with a good kick.

He put the phone in her hand while he searched the floor for his pants and left her to check her messages.

"The first one is from Detective Wong," she said aloud before her message service connected. She put the phone on speaker and set the phone down.

"This is Detective Wong. I wanted to call you with an update. The man we have in custody gave us some interesting information. After the shooting, his boss cut him loose, but he gave us the address for the man's headquarters. We went there to serve a warrant, but the office was empty. The house that was connected to them was empty as well. From everything we can find the other shooter and their boss have left the islands.

"We believe that they fled to avoid prosecution. We're still

processing the two locations, hoping to find some fingerprints or other evidence to learn their identities, but so far the names we have for both of the men came up with nothing.

"No birth certificates, valid licenses. I want to caution you that all of this information is what we have at the moment. If you have any questions, you know how to get a hold of me, but I want to let you know that as of this moment the official position of the HPD is that you're not in any immediate danger."

"Not in any immediate danger." Hi`ilani repeated the words to herself as if she was speaking a foreign language and was trying to sound it out and trying to decipher its meaning. "Not in any immediate danger."

Jackson pulled a t-shirt over his head and walked around to her side of the bed.

Pulling her up onto her feet, he wrapped his arms around her. "Thank God."

She sighed and relaxed into his arms.

When she leaned back, she looked up at him. "Suddenly," she smiled, "I'm starving."

"Then let's feed you." He was leaning in for a kiss when she put her hands in the center of his chest and held him back.

"Let's feed your guys too. I'm afraid to tell them they came back early for nothing without a good meal in their stomachs."

He couldn't help the smile on his lips. "I think you're going to get along great with them if you keep trying to feed them."

Sitting in the back corner of L & L's Hawaiian Barbeque, Hi`ilani was having a hard time actually eating her lunch. She'd been listening to the men talking about their adventures on leave and enjoying every minute of it.

And every time she'd tried to apologize to Baron and Train for the SOS that had brought them back, they waved it off. And in Train's case, he focused on something else entirely.

Flirting outrageously.

"Don't you think it's only fair," he leaned his forearms on the table, "that I get a chance to woo the fair maiden before she settles for the wrong man?"

Hi`ilani laughed and felt the hand that Jackson had settled on the back of her chair grip the wooden frame a little too hard. Leaning closer to him, touching her shoulder to his chest, she set her hand on his knee. "Breathe, Jack. I'm not taking him seriously."

Train's smile didn't dim in the least, nor did he seem to see the hard look in Jackson's eyes. "That would be his mistake, beautiful."

Jackson's thigh tensed under her hand and while she worried that he was a few blithe comments away from strangling his friend, she had to admit she was a little turned on.

Okay, more than a little.

It was less than an hour ago that those thigh muscles had helped to make her scream into his pillow.

Baron had no problem tucking into his food. When he looked up at Jackson he sat back in his chair and grabbed a napkin, wiping a bit of gravy off of his lip. "Seriously, Ajax. Train's just trying to get you to lose your cool. Up until now you were icy calm most of the time." He looked across at Hi`ilani. "That was my choice for his nickname, you know. Ice-man."

Train jumped into the conversation with both feet. "But it started a bit of an argument. Some of the guys thought it was because of the X-men, you know the guy with the wings?"

Baron smacked him on the shoulder. "The guy who could turn things to ice. The guy with the wings is called Angel."

"Sure, whatever." Train shrugged, leaning closer to Hi`ilani. "She's the angel around here." He leaned back when Jackson laid his forearm on the table top. "And the other guys thought it was because of... of..."

"Top Gun?" Hi`ilani wanted to help and reach for her soda.

"Top Gun!" Train repeated with a big grin. "Yes!" He intercepted her hand and leaned forward to kiss it. "Ow!"

Lowering her hand back down to the table, Train bent over to the side and rubbed his leg.

He glared up at Baron. "What did you do that for?"

"Saving your hide." Baron rolled his eyes. "What do you think it would do to your reputation if Ajax killed you with a plastic knife?"

Train sighed and sat back up and looked at Hi`ilani. "But Top Gun is connected to the Navy, so that wasn't going to work."

"No," she took a sip of her soda through the straw, "I guess it wouldn't."

"What do they call this again?" Baron pointed down at his plate.

Hi`ilani looked over at his plate. "Loco Moco."

Train smiled. His family came from Spain way back in his family tree. Efrain Figueroa was a name that appeared every few generations in his family tree. "Crazy?"

She shrugged. "I'm not sure of the origin of it exactly. But it seems more like a contraction of Local to Loco and Moco probably just rhymed with it."

Baron stared down at his plate. "I'm getting used to all the sticky rice here in Hawaii, but you give me a burger patty, a couple of over easy eggs and gravy? I'm all about this kind of food."

Hi`ilani was still laughing at the smile on Baron's normally serious face when her phone rang. She started to excuse herself to answer it, but Train waved her back into her seat.

"If you want to go outside one of us will go with you."

Rolling her eyes she answered the phone. It didn't make sense to drag one of them outside. Besides they were the only ones in the place at this point in the day.

"Hey, CeeCee. What's up?"

The answer was so loud she had to lean way from the phone for a moment. When CeeCee got over her first rush of screams she lowered her tone and spoke so that the dogs didn't hear her.

Hi`ilani listened as her agent filled her in on the pertinent details.

"Okay. I'll check my email. Yes, I don't think we'll have a problem. Detective Wong says everything should be okay now... yes, yes... okay. I'll check. Okay. Yes. Okay. Fine. Yes. Thanks, CeeCee... now go take a breath. Maybe lie down for a few minutes or so? Okay, love you too. Bye-bye."

"Wow," Train laughed, a full-throated laugh that had the lady behind the counter tittering behind her hand, "that woman can talk!"

"You mean," she returned, "she can scream. CeeCee is like the battery bunny in those commercials. She just can't stop herself."

Jackson leaned into her side. "So… what's the thing she called about."

She knew her cheeks were flushed with color and she wasn't sure exactly how to broach the subject with him. "Well, awhile back when I had a bunch of time on my hands." She looked away from Jackson for a moment. She didn't want to tell him that she had most of that time because they'd stopped seeing each other. "And while that was going on, CeeCee sent me to some auditions for commercials and things. I got a small part in a local film and the director made me a tape out of my scenes. CeeCee sent it out to casting agents."

She could see Train getting more excited by the minute, but she couldn't read Baron's expression. And Jackson, well, she couldn't see him and didn't want to turn to look up at him, afraid he'd think it was something crazy.

"I don't know if you heard of that new show that they're going to film here starting in the summer. Honolulu P.I."

"I have!" Train smacked the table top. "Are you going to be on that?"

Hi`ilani nodded. "I have a reoccurring character that

might change depending how I do in the first half of the season and if we get picked up for a second."

She let out a breath.

"So, CeeCee was calling to find out if I can make the press conference."

"Press conference?" Train was seriously going to get himself in trouble with Jackson if he didn't stop staring at her like that.

"There's a local fan convention. Like Comic Con, but it covers all kinds of stuff… anything that has fans. The Network wants to introduce the cast at the con. When all of this happened with Mackie the press event was still just an idea, but now they've scheduled time."

"Hey."

She felt Jackson's hand on her shoulder and she turned to look up at him.

"What's got you so worried?"

"I know that Detective Wong said everything looked okay. That the other men responsible are gone, but I wasn't sure what you'd say. Or if you'd even be excited for me and-"

He leaned down into her, slanting his lips against her for a kiss. Her gasp only deepened the kiss and when he pulled back, she was starry-eyed and speechless.

"Baby, I'm so proud of you I might actually act like Train for the rest of the day."

She laughed and felt all the worry on her shoulder slide away.

Jackson's words continued to comfort her. "And you're going to be at that… that, whatever you call it. I'm going to make sure you're safe while you're there."

Train jumped in. "Oh, there is no way you're going to keep me out of it."

Hi`ilani looked across at Train. "I wouldn't dare tell you no."

Baron swallowed the last bite of his lunch and picked up his bottled water. "And I'm going too. Better safe than sorry."

Sato sat down on the sofa in his new office and stared out the glass window at the topless bar across the street. "Oh, how the mighty have fallen."

Peck set down a box and gave his boss a look.

Smiling, Sato looked at him. "We still have boxes in the truck."

He saw the way a muscle ticked in Peck's jaw. He wasn't going to push the man much more. They were both upset. Both of them frustrated.

But, as the adage went, the shit rolls downhill and Peck was downhill. "Let's get the rest of the boxes up here."

Peck headed for the door and stopped. "A little help?"

Sato's goodwill, what he had of it, was fading quickly. "I'm waiting for a call."

He almost didn't care if Peck understood the point of the comment. Still, it would be good for the man to remember who was the head guy around here. Muscle is good, but to get where he was in his life, in this business, it took being ruthless and cold.

Peck would only last as long as it served him.

The gunman nodded and walked out the door into the hallway and kicked it shut with his foot.

"Well, that was uncalled for." A few moments later his phone rang and he picked it up. "You're late," he grumbled. "You're going to lose money because of that, and you're not going to argue. We have a… mutual acquaintance, and I think he's lonely in lockup. Poor boy couldn't make bail.

"I want to remind everyone how generous I can be." He smiled and leaned back on the sofa, lifting one leg to set it over the other, making the sunlight gleam off the side of his highly-polished Oxfords. "I'd like you to make sure he's not lonely anymore."

Jackson didn't mind waiting in the lobby of the Diamond Head Studios. There was more than enough to look at while the cast was doing their first read through. The room had a number of comfortable chairs that told him people regularly spent a good amount of time here.

The walls were a veritable museum of pictures and some notable props from shows and movies that had shared the soundstage or Diamond Head Studios property. It had already been a couple of hours, but none of that mattered to him.

He was waiting for one particular moment and given

the crescendo of sound near the doors and the shift of light visible through the crack under the heavy metal.

Standing up from the chair he'd just started to settle in.

When the doors opened a few people walked out, talking amongst themselves. He wasn't as into movies and TV as Train was, but he thought he might actually recognize a few of the faces. Still, he couldn't put names to the faces. Train would probably pester him and show him the whole cast on that movie information website he trolled like it was his job.

"Hey!"

He saw Hi`ilani's hand waving above the heads of the exiting crowd.

As soon the slightest path opened up, he saw her, but he didn't move toward her, he just stood there and watched.

She was, in a word, amazing.

Graceful in every move. Talented beyond his understanding.

And if the dark-haired man beside her didn't take his hand away from her shoulders, Jackson was probably going to end up in trouble. Even when she moved straight to him, the man didn't give up his place beside her, and his eyes, well they were more than just curious. The man was clearly interested.

"Jack, this is Cort Caldwell. He's going to be the lead in the show." She turned to the side. "Cort, this is Jackson Guard." As they shook each other's hand, Jackson couldn't help but smile as Hi`ilani moved up beside him and wrapped her arm around his waist. "Jackson's my boyfriend."

That took the wind out of the actor's sails and Jackson had to tamp down his smile so it wouldn't look so smug.

Cort excused himself and another gentleman stepped outside, moving toward Hi`ilani with a big grin. He looked like a proud papa when he took Hi`ilani's hand and pressed a kiss to her fingers.

"You, my dear, are going to be a star."

Jackson could see her cheeks flush with color.

"I just want to make sure you don't regret casting me."

"Never! In fact, I was a little late coming out because I had a little meeting with the head writer. They're going to add more to your part. You've got great chemistry with Cort," they both heard Hi`ilani gasp in shock, "and I think if we gave your scenes the right snark and sass it could be like… Moonlighting."

Jackson knew he was going to have to look that show up.

"Thank you, Mr. Hutchins! Oh!" She looked up at Jackson, I forgot to introduce you."

"I can manage that." Chuckling, Mr. Hutchins extended his hand to Jackson. "Jim Hutchins, I'm the Executive Producer of Honolulu P.I. And from what I understand you wanted to speak to me."

Jackson shook his hand, admiring the man's firm grip. "Yes, sir. I just wanted to make sure that the upcoming press event is safe."

Jim looked him up and down, nodding. "Military?"

"Yes, sir." Jackson's mouth tilted up at a corner.

Again, Jim looked at him, narrowing his eyes for a moment before he stepped back and nodded. "Army?"

With the barest hint of a chuckle, Jackson nodded. "Yes, sir."

Jim gestured down the hall. "Why don't you both come with me into this office and we can chat for a moment."

Jackson made sure to step behind Hi`ilani and follow behind the to, keeping a watch on the doorway behind them through the reflection in the opposite glass doors.

When he entered the room, the producer had already pulled a chair out for Hi`ilani and settled her in it.

He was quickly beginning to like the man. It didn't seem like he was doing it just for effect. And when Jackson explained the situation that had led up to their meeting, Mr. Hutchins listened careful and offered his condolences to Hi`ilani.

"But the Detective doesn't think it's going to be a problem?"

Jackson heard the man's hopeful tone and he didn't blame him. "That's what he said," he reached out a hand and Hi`ilani held it in both of hers, settling it in her lap, "but I hope you'll understand that I'm more than a little concerned. This sudden disappearance makes me more nervous than relieved."

Watching him carefully, Jim Hutchins thought through the words. "I can see what you're saying. Hmm..." He gave Hi`ilani a gentle smile. "I would be concerned as well. They have one of the men in custody, but since there were two shooters I can't imagine that having one on the hook to pay for the loss of your friend would be enough."

Turning back to Jackson he leaned an arm on the edge

of the table. "Your worry probably won't amount to much. Fighting local crime is in the hands of the HPD. Still, the room we have for the con is the biggest one and from the social media buzz, we'll likely be standing room only for the event."

Pulling out his phone he typed out a message that took up a bunch of lines on the screen. Once he sent it he let both of them know. "I've messaged my assistant. She'll have an HPI Staff badge for you to access the room without having to wait in line." He chuckled. "But that doesn't mean that people will give you space. Fans at these cons are loathe to give up a good space while they have it."

"Thank you, Sir." Jackson blew out a breath. "I hate to ask but two of my teammates are coming with me. Would it be possible to get three badges? We can cover the back-stage area and two in the house."

The producer thought through his words and Jackson had more than a passing appreciation for the older man. "We also have hired some HPD officers for security. We have quiet a few well-known actors cast in the show so we will be expecting a crush in the room.

"You won't be allowed to bring weapons in, but I'll provide you with the passes. Will that be enough?"

Jackson knew it was as good as he could expect, especially if Detective Wong thought everything was going to be just fine. "I would appreciate that, sir."

"Great!" Jim looked at Hi`ilani and gave her an encouraging smile. "Between HPD and your man here," he nodded, "you'll be just fine."

"Thank you, sir."

"You don't need to thank me, sweetheart. We're all going to be family and we take care of each other."

&

Hi`ilani handed a clean plate to Train and rolled her eyes at him when he gave her a wink.

Pausing as he was scrubbing a plate clean beside her, Jackson sighed at his friend. "Will you stop flirting with my girlfriend!"

"I'm not flirting." Turning the plate in his hands over, Train continued wiping the plate dry. "I'm just expressing my gratitude that she's rinsing. My hands turn to prunes in minutes."

"And that," sighed Baron as he read the paper at the kitchen counter, "is why you would have made a crappy SEAL."

Train shrugged. "I can't help that I look so good in swim trunks, but actually swimming is not my favorite thing."

Hi`ilani had to blink her eyes to clear them of her tears. "Are you guys this much fun every day?"

"These guys?' Jackson jerked a thumb back at Baron.

"Yeah, is this what you guys are always like?"

Train jumped in to answer. "Baron's always grumpy," he agreed, "but he's a big Monty Python fan so sometimes even when he's joking we don't know and think he's just being a jerk."

That was confusing. "Then what does Monty Python have to do with any of it?"

Jackson leaned closer and pressed a kiss to her temple.

"It's the only kind of humor he can deliver and make it seem almost humorous." He thought for a moment and then added on, "Unless it's SPAM or I'm a Lumberjack. He's been banned from singing that around the rest of us."

Baron sat back in his chair and slapped the newspaper down on the hard surface. "It was only at Halloween! And it was my costume!"

Train held up his hands to placate Baron. "Yes, yes… we know… relax."

Hi`ilani felt Jackson's hand on her shoulder.

"You look like you're about to cry."

She smiled up at him. "If anything, it's happy tears. Don't get me wrong, I love my apartment, but it's surprisingly quiet most of the time. It's going to be hard to get used to it again."

Jackson took hold of her shoulders and crouched down enough to look straight into her eyes. "What are you saying?"

She looked down at first, willing her heartbeat to maintain an easy, friendly pace within her chest. "I feel like a fourth wheel around here. You guys need your space and I'm fine going back on my own.

"I'm sure I'm a pretty decent buzzkill for three bachelors living together."

She heard the cessation in conversation between the other two but couldn't quite meet their eyes.

"I'm thinking after the press event, when we know more from Detective Wong, it'll probably be a good time to move back to Waikiki."

"Whoa, hey," Train shrugged off Baron's hold and

made it to her side. "Don't way that! With you here Baron doesn't walk around naked all the time."

In answer, Baron smacked Train hard enough on the back that the other man staggered forward a couple of steps.

"Okay, so many it's not naked, but I swear I saw a g-string."

Baron's eyes were dark and filled with warning. "Those were… a friend's."

Train winked a Hi`ilani. "Friend in this case means 'lady friend.'"

Grabbing Train by the scruff of his neck, Baron started to move the man across the room. When they stopped outside of the first bedroom, Baron turned around and gave her smile. "Don't leave on my account. You're kind of nice to have around."

"Kind of?"

For his question, Train managed to duck and miss most of Baron's blow, glancing off the back of his head.

"Come on, you can finish the dishes later."

Train moved along for a bit and then stopped short to look at Baron. "Why do I have to finish the dishes?"

By the time the other two disappeared into their rooms to give the couple a little privacy. She could see that Jackson was ready for a fight.

"I need to know you're safe."

She nodded. "You don't think this thing is over yet."

"Do you?" He wanted her opinion more than anything.

She thought about it and then shook her head. "It seems too easy, doesn't it?"

He sighed. "I'm not trying to make you worry, or make

you afraid, but if something happened to you and I didn't say something or try to stop it. I'd never forgive myself."

"I'm not asking you to." She heard the tremor in his voice and felt the hiccup in her own heartbeat. "Do you think I should call and cancel the event?"

"No!"

The vehemence in his voice shocked her.

It sounded almost pained.

He pulled her close and turned so her back was up against the counter. "No, you don't have to give up this event, Hi`i. This is a huge break for you and I wouldn't ask you to give it up."

She felt tears on her lashes. "That's just it. It's big for me but if I go and something happens and someone else is hurt for me. I don't think I could handle it. I'm… I'm still not sure that Mackie's death wasn't my fault. Everyone tells me that it wasn't, but I can't escape the feeling that if I hadn't gone out there, they wouldn't have had a reason to shoot him."

He picked her up and set her up on the counter. "No one is responsible for what the shooters did, except for the shooters. Mackie did what he did because he loved you. Those men did what they did because they wanted to."

"I'm going to be in a roomful of people. Innocent people. And if something happens-"

"You're going to have me. You're going to have Baron and Train there too. They might act like little children sometimes, but I trust them with my life and I trust them with yours."

He set his palms down on either side of her on the counter and leaned in.

Closing her eyes, she breathed in his scent. She felt his heat surrounding her.

His strength.

She felt him rub his cheek against hers.

"And there's one more thing working in our favor."

That caught his attention and he leaned back enough that she opened her eyes to look up at him. He was watching her carefully. "And what's that?"

"Mister Hutchins said we'll have the HPD there. You never know," she lifted up her chin in a little defiant gesture, "Kyle might be there and- Oh!"

Jackson wrapped his arms around her, his hands grabbing the full curve of her backside and pulled her to the edge of the counter.

Before he could speak, she rolled her hips against him and she felt him hardening against her.

"So, I'm guessing you don't want me to talk about Ky-"

His hands lifted her off of the counter completely and with a soft gasp she wrapped herself around him, arms and legs and when she smiled at him with a wink he covered her mouth with a kiss.

When he came up for air she murmured against his lips. "So, I guess that's a no."

He swept the tip of his tongue along her bottom lip. "I'm going to get you to say yes in a minute… to me."

She arched against him, rubbing her breasts against his chest. "Make me."

Hi`ilani laughed against his lips as he carried her away.

CHAPTER 15

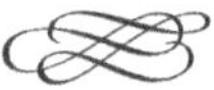

Honolulu Fan Con could be described by one word: PACKED.

If anyone of the group was expected to enjoy the event, it would have been Train. If they'd known him a little longer before they gave him his nickname they might have ended up calling him Telenovella.

But even as much as he enjoyed TV and movies, after a few minutes of trying to move through the throngs at the Hawaii Convention Center, even Train was soured on the idea. "Did they have a back entrance?"

Baron was decided chipper, putting his teammates off balance. "Nope, but this is kind of interesting. People watching," he mused, "who would have thought I might enjoy something like this."

Train glared at him. "I think I'm going to hate you for a while."

Baron shrugged and pointed forward. "Keep your eyes up ahead."

As they made their way down the hallway, a rather

frazzled looking production assistant waved them forward. "Come on through."

The four of them stepped through the doorway and took a deep breath of fresh air. Train stretched his arms out wide. "How many people are out there?"

The production assistant, not realizing it was a rhetorical question piped up and gave them a dazzling grin. "At last count at the gate there are more than nine thousand people in the building."

"Fuck."

At least Baron was back to his usual jolly self.

Jackson walked Hi`ilani over to Mr. Hutchins. He greeted her with a big hug and shook Jackson's hand.

With a curious look at the solider, Mr. Hutchins watched Jackson's eyes carefully as he gave him a hesitant poke in his chest. Then all five fingers, nodding to himself when he confirmed that there was a bullet proof vest under his shirt. "Interesting."

Cort sidled up to the side and leaned in, intending to press a kiss on Hi`ilani's cheek.

She stepped aside and smiled at him. "Hey, Cort."

The actor shrugged. "Can't blame a guy for trying, right?"

Jim put a hand on Cort's shoulder. "Cort, a word of advice."

Cort shrugged. "Okay?"

Jim gestured at Hi`ilani first. "When a woman sidesteps a kiss, that's a pretty good indicator that she's not comfortable with what you're doing."

"Well, you said we're probably going to be involved on the show."

From his place a few steps over, Train folded his arms over his chest. "That's in front of the camera," he explained in a tone that said he didn't think he had to, "off-camera you pay attention before someone makes you pay attention."

Jim gave Train a nodding smile. "Couldn't have said it better myself, son." He gestured to Jackson and the other two men. "You know Jackson's her boyfriend, but go ahead and test the limits of his patience and the least of your worries is going to be the black eye he gives you."

Cort leaned back. "You'd let him punch me?"

Jim leaned closer, lowering his voice. "And then there's going to be the harassment suit. The network won't stand for it and I won't stand for it. So, get your act together, Cort."

As Jim walked away, shaking his head, he called out to no one in particular, "Can someone get Cort some coffee?"

The production assistant scooted around Cort, her eyes watchful, but she walked up to Hi`ilani and the guys. "Our Public Relations manager wanted me to let you know that the house is open so if you guys want to go and find seats out in the hall, now is the time."

Hi`ilani reached her arms around Jackson's neck and gave him a quick kiss to his lips. "After this is over I can't wait to get you alone and-"

"Ahem."

They turned and saw Train and Baron pointing at their ears. Train gave them both a wry smile. "Ajax has his earpiece on."

She stepped away from Jackson and he pulled her back for another quick peck on her lips.

"We'll finish this later."

Baron groaned. "Will you just go before I die of sugar shock?"

Train jogged up and brushed a kiss on her cheek before he moved up to Jackson's side.

"All right," she looked at Baron, "you're stuck with me."

Baron slung and arm around her shoulders and gave her an awkward hug. "I think you know by now you're the one that's stuck with me. Now," he let out a sigh as Cort grabbed a bunch of donuts and headed for a chair, "let's keep you away from 'grab-ass' over there and we'll review the plans we worked out earlier."

"You've got to be more careful, Baron."

His eyes narrowed at her. "Why?"

She looked up at him with a sly smile. "You keep acting like this and people are going to think you're actually nice."

Shaking his head, he growled at her. "Let's just keep that between us, okay?"

Shrugging, she moved toward the stage with Baron at her side.

Even with their earpieces turned up on full. Jackson was having a hard time hearing anything more than the excited conversations around him. The press event was set just after the lunch hour and people were packed in shoulder to shoulder in the room and a quick look at the two doors at the back of the room it looked like they were still letting people in.

Train Here I thought I'd enjoy coming to this Con.

Baron Does that mean we don't have to hear you going on and on about movies and TV?

Train Kiss my-

Ajax Focus, you two.

Train All right, Mr. Miyaji.

Baron I can look through the curtain. Does the Fire Marshal know how many people they are squeezing in here?

Train Oh good. They just closed the doors.

❧

Hi`ilani waited in order behind the curtain. Baron was standing just off to the side. Once everyone was announced and seated, he'd remain behind the curtain, but he'd be right behind her just in case.

In case.

Living with these worries was starting to wear on her.

Then again, Jackson lived like this all the time. She'd only had a taste of the kind of preparation that the men went through. Sitting around their dining room table, the surface had been covered in schematics and information sheets. They'd planned and planned again. They'd come up with several solid plans to use in case something happened at the con.

"Hey."

She turned to see Baron turn off his earpiece for a moment. "Yeah?"

"You okay? Ready for this?"

Hi`ilani shook her head. "Not in the least." She saw him open his mouth to speak but she rushed right over him, trying to awkwardly reassure him. "I'm totally confident in the three of you. I'm just worried I'm going to freeze up and put someone in danger if something happens."

A flash of an image in her head, a memory of Mackie, brought tears to her eyes.

"You don't worry at all." Baron set his hand on her shoulder and gave her a squeeze so gentle she was shocked. "If something happens, know that I will take care of you. Do you trust us to keep you safe?"

She dropped her chin in a nod. "Absolutely."

Cort heard his name and stepped through the opening in the curtain and was greeted by a huge round of applause.

The production assistant that they'd met earlier didn't seem phased in the least by her tears and handed Hi`ilani a tissue, giving her a big smile. "Head up, you'll be just fine."

Hi`ilani heard Jim announcing her, but honestly the words weren't more than just a jumble of sounds. In the back of her head she knew what was being said, CeeCee had read it to her a few times over the phone. Honestly it didn't matter what they said, she was afraid that the audience would know she was a nobody and there would be crickets after her introduction.

But she was wrong.

Stepping out into the brightly lit stage she was stunned to see the crowd on its feet cheering for her.

To say she was stunned was an understatement and it took her a moment to feel the world under her feet again. Lifting a hand she waved at the crowd and the applause rose into a crescendo again.

Hi`ilani wiped at the tears on her cheeks and found her seat at the table.

While Jim was adding a few more comments, she couldn't help but reach out and pick up the tent card that had her name on it and turned it around to look at it.

Hi`ilani Ahfong

Wow.

"Hi`ilani?"

Realizing that Jim was calling her name she dropped the tent car back into the table and looked over at him. "Sorry. I'm still trying to believe all of this…"

&a.

Jackson watched her from the audience when he could. Most of the time he was scanning the audience. They didn't know what the other gunman looked like. And they didn't know if the boss was there. It wasn't likely, but men who do what they did, didn't make too much sense to begin with.

Evil tended to make people feel invincible.

It was the innocents that suffered and Hi`ilani was as innocent as they come. She lived with her heart on her sleeve and her spirit was full of love. Aloha.

The word did indeed mean a whole host of things, but Hi`ilani embodied so many of them.

Someone shifted in the crowd and his head turned in their direction, finding a thin man, tall enough to see him over the crowd. He was reaching into a messenger bag slung over his shoulder.

Ajax Hold, possible target.

When he pulled out an old SLR camera, Jackson relax, stretching his neck to ease some of the tension.

Ajax Negative.

Train Okay, nothing here so far.

Baron She's holding up well.

Jackson felt a well of pride in his heart.

Ajax Of course she is. Pay attention.

He knew that he'd failed at putting an edge in his tone. He couldn't feel the way he felt and not smile.

❦

A young woman stepped up to the microphone set up for audience questions. Leaning closer until there was about an inch between her mouth and the surface. "I have a question for Hi`ilani?"

Jim nodded. "Go ahead."

She lifted a hand and waved, the headband she wore had two Daleks from Doctor Who attached by little springs. "Aloha, Hi`ilani! My name is Kimi." She giggled. "I've been a fan of your music since I heard you at the House Without a Key restaurant."

Hi`ilani leaned forward. "Mahalo, Kimi! Thanks for being a fan."

"My heart is pounding!" Kimi flattened her hand over her heart. "I wanted to ask if we're going to get to hear you sing and see you dance on the show."

Hi`ilani looked at Jim and he gestured for her to answer.

"Well, we just did the first read through of the Pilot script and I do have a scene in it where you'll see a little bit of both."

Kimi clapped her hands and did a little dance in place.

"So awesome! Can't wait!"

The next question was for Cort and he made a big show of leaning on the table and smiling at the beaming woman behind the microphone.

"Hey there, I'm Denise and I'm a huge fan of yours, Cort."

He winked at her. "Good to know, Denise. I love meeting fans."

"And I would love to meet you later." She fanned herself and more than a few people in the audience made little appreciative noises and whistles. At a polite gesture from one of the staff members she jumped into asking her question. "Do you have a love interest that we'll see develop over a number of episodes or will you have a long line of one night stands on the show?" She paused for a second and then burst out again. "And if it's the second, where do I volunteer?"

Laughter filtered through the audience and someone grumbled through the communications link. Jackson wasn't at all sure that it hadn't been him.

Cort, shifted on stage and got up from his chair. "Well, I probably shouldn't say this much-"

"Then please, don't." Jim's tone was pretty pointed when he spoke into the microphone.

"But I think it's safe to say that I know I would love to see something develop between my character and," he extended a hand toward Hi`ilani, "this beautiful woman right here."

Baron Jerk.

Train If you want, Ajax. I can break a few of his fingers for you.

Jackson laughed quietly.

Ajax I'm not worried. If he tries something, then you can help me break his kneecaps.

Baron I'd aim a little higher, but that's just me.

Ajax I love you, man.

Baron Kisses.

&

Hi`ilani smiled even though she wanted to stomp on Cort's foot. The man wasn't going to let it go.

Sliding a quick look down the table she saw more than a few of the cast members trying to hide their own reactions to Cort's behavior.

Jim, at his end of the table looked like he was one comment away from smoke pouring out of his ears.

"What about you, Hi`ilani?"

She shook herself and realized that it was Cort asking the question.

"Don't you want to see how hot our chemistry can burn?"

It took everything she had not to roll her eyes.

Reaching forward, she pulled her microphone closer and tried to find the right words.

"Well, this is Hawaii. Just because things get hot, it doesn't mean it'll be good. Just look at the people who sun bathe in Waikiki without sunscreen. That's a painful burn."

More than a few people laughed in the audience. She turned to look at the crowd and had to blink a few times when she saw what looked like dozens of flashes from cameras.

The light had an odd effect on her eyes, making spots of her vision lighter but others darker. At first it was just disconcerting and then it threw her back in time.

To a night in a darkened park.

And there, in the midst of the all of the happy, smiling faces in the audience, there was one that made her blood run cold.

Tall, blond, his eyes as cold as his jaw was square.

Her breathing sped up as her heart squeezed tight.

She couldn't hear anything or see anything else but his face.

And the blood rushing through her ears.

She should call out.

She should point at him.

Do something!

The only thing that seemed to work besides her eyes were her legs.

Standing, she pushed the chair back from the table and she took a step back, her knees buckling when the backs of her legs came in contact with the chair.

Jackson saw the change in Hi`ilani. Felt a tremor of fear roll through his body when he saw her stand up and back away from the table.

His first instinct was to wade through the crowd and put himself between her and danger, but his job was to find the danger and leave her safety to Baron.

Ajax Train?

Train Moving toward the middle.

He felt the movement before he saw it. He had to watch the crowd, look for cues. There. The gunman acted like a rock dropped into a pond. He straightened up, lifting his arms and the people around him leaned away, looking for a way out.

Ajax I see him. Polo shirt black. Tan pants.

Train Got him. Closing in.

Jackson was the man, Ajax was the soldier and it was Ajax that waded through the crowd, moving people out of the way as he kept his focus on the man who'd helped to kill Mackie.

The man who intended to kill Hi`ilani.

And the only thing Ajax knew was that the man would fail.

He'd do whatever it took to stop him.

When he was a couple of feet away he saw Train approaching from the other side and knew before Train even moved what his friend was going to do.

"Hey!"

The gunman spared him a glance but turned back to the stage, determined to finish the job.

Jackson's hip bumped into a chair and he used it to his advantage. Putting a boot on the seat, he used the upholstered chair to launch himself into the air.

He drove the man to the ground a split second after the gun went off.

Train was beside him a moment later, stomping his boot on the man's hand and prying the gun from his finger. "Got him, Ajax?"

"Yes," he growled the word through his clenched teeth. "I've got him."

Beneath him, the man struggled, trying to buck him off. His size would have given him an advantage if there hadn't been the red hot rage surging through his blood.

Ajax Baron, sit rep

Baron Safe

Ajax Thank you

Baron Whatever

Someone put a hand on Jackson's shoulder. "Back up."

Jackson tensed and kept his grip on the man's wrist that he'd twisted behind his back.

Train HPD

Pressing his knee into the back of the shooter's thigh, Jackson held out his hand, palm up. "Cuffs."

"We'll do that. Move."

Jackson saw the glint in the shooter's eye as he glared up at him. He was just waiting for a chance.

When Jackson shook his head he didn't allow for an

argument. "He's waiting for an opening. Give me the cuffs and then you guys can have him."

He waited for an argument from the officer. So did Train. His teammate's eyes spoke volumes.

"Here, take mine."

Jackson looked up over Train's shoulders and saw Kyle Ballard in his HPD uniform. He was working the event. The look in his eyes said he wouldn't have been too disappointed if Jackson had been the one on his stomach under a couple of well-placed knees and restraining hands, but still he was offering his cuffs.

That was probably the most that he could ever hope for.

He gave the officer a nod and took the cuffs from him. "Thanks."

Kyle stepped back as Jackson snapped the cuffs around the man's wrist, and then together, he and Train managed to pull his other arm behind his back.

An officer took possession of the sidearm and once the two Deltas had him up on his feet they surrendered him to the officers.

Before anyone could stop them, they rushed through the crowd toward the backstage area. The last thing they heard as they pushed through the heavy metal door at the back of the room was applause.

&

Hi`ilani waited, watching the door to the room as if it was the only thing keeping her sane.

And maybe it was.

And maybe it was Baron's hold on her arm.

"He's fine," Baron's tone wasn't his usual growl but it wasn't soft either. If he'd been sweet, she would have dissolved into tears.

"I know," her voice was barely a whisper. She knew he was okay. She just had to see it for herself.

The door swung open and her knees went weak, but that didn't stop her from running into his arms.

Jackson picked her up and held her to him as he robbed her of oxygen and the last remnants of fear.

CHAPTER 16

Sitting on the lanai at the back of Jackson's house with Baron manning the grill, more like appropriating the grill, the others took up all the available furniture with part of the group including Hi`ilani, Jackson and Rayne sitting on thick *zabuton* pillows on the floor.

Mary sighed as a soft breeze blew through the shaded space. "I still can't believe we missed it all!"

Rayne shook her head at her friend and continued to copy Hi`ilani's movements as they both made *haku* leis out of flowers and croton leaves from Jackson's yard. "I'm actually happy we weren't there for a shooting, but from what we heard your guys had everything well in hand."

Ghost looked over at Jackson and took a quick sip of his beer before he spoke. "Just how did you get through the crowd and up to the stage?"

"It wasn't me. My job was to get to the shooter." Jackson looked back at the other team leader and shook his head. Reaching out, Jackson touched his hand to Hi`ilani's back, reassuring himself that she was there with him. "I saw the fear on her face and I knew the gunman was in the crowd. I had to get to him and take him down."

"And you did," she leaned against him and turned to brush a kiss on his shoulders. "And then Baron swept me off my feet."

Mary sighed and laughed. "So did you give Baron a kiss!"

The man in question groaned from his place at the grill. "I didn't want to hurt the boy's feelings so I kept my lips to myself."

Truck's laughter was louder than everyone else. "I almost wish we could stay for your next hand to hand combat training. I'm sure Ajax is going to enjoy ripping you apart, B."

"He's got nothing to worry about." Train gave Hi`ilani a wink. "Ajax swept you off your feet in that service hallway at the back of the room. All they needed was some orchestral music and a fade out to make it perfect."

Jackson gave his friend a look. "It was perfect just the way it was."

Train waved him off. "Well, if you want to see the rescue for yourself," Train added as he quickly searched a browser on his phone, "there were no less than two hundred camera phones in the audience. TMZ picked up this video." Train turned his phone around and put it in Ghost's hand.

"It made for great TV and online fodder," Baron scoffed as he prodded a steak with his barbeque tongs.

Ghost watched the video and then looked down under the window. "It's got more than two million views and going up by the minute."

Hi`ilani winced at the thought. "The best part about it was that after Train and Jack had him pinned down, the special duty HPD officers took him into custody they got him to talk. Turns out the prosecutor pointed out that being responsible for the death of a well-loved local performer wasn't going to make him popular at O-Triple-C."

Jackson nodded. "The local inmates would take their anger out on his hide."

Nodding, Hi`ilani continued. "So he made a deal to give up his boss and enough evidence to send him to prison for the rest of his life, in exchange for a chance to serve his sentence somewhere on the continent. Now they have to try to find their boss and bring him to justice. Somehow, I don't think it's going to be that easy."

"Sorry we couldn't do more to help." Train took the phone that Ghost handed back to him and tucked it away in his pocket. "What did the producers say about the whole thing?"

Hi`ilani's shoulders shook with a little embarrassed shrug. "They didn't fire me, that's for sure. Still, someone floated a story that it was just a stunt exhibition from the show."

Truck chuckled. "Someone's got a spin master working for the network. Good cover story."

"And it takes the pressure off of Hi`ilani. She can just start her work on the show and enjoy the hell out of it!" Mary laid back against Truck's chest and sighed. "But what a great story to tell your kids when they ask about how you met and fell in love."

Her cheeks flushed with color, Hi`ilani added another

flower to the lei, holding it down with her thumb while she started to wind the raffia around the central part of the lei. "It has a fairytale kind of feel to it… after the shooting, that is."

"Fairytales?" Baron groused from the grill. "Does that mean that we're the dwarves, I refuse to wear tights."

Train gave him a look. "Just cook your meat and stop grumbling."

Handing a flower to Rayne, Hi`ilani nodded at her progress. "You're doing great!"

Rayne beamed at the praise and the look she shared with Ghost did a fair job of warming the air around everyone.

Trying to let them have their moment, Hi`ilani reached down for another blossom and came up empty. Leaning to the side she touched the mat underneath her pillow and sighed. "Jack?"

Leaning forward, he kissed her cheek. "Yeah?"

"Can you get more flowers for us?"

"Ha!" Baron pointed his tongs at the two of them. "Whipped! So whipped!"

"Mind your own business, meat boy!" Train turned back around and grinned at her. "That'll keep him quiet for a minute."

Hi`ilani turned and almost looked over her shoulder at Jack. She touched his thigh and gave it a reassuring pat. "No need, Jack, I'll clip this off and go pick some-"

"Here," he kissed her bare shoulder, "hold out your hand."

Rolling her eyes, she held out her hand and waited for him to put a flower in her palm.

The cool metal against her skin made her gasp.

She brought her hand closer and looked down.

"A ring." It wasn't just any ring. It was a white gold ring with a beautiful diamond at the center and the sides were carved in beautiful scrollwork with black enamel that was the quintessential characteristic of Hawaiian Jewelry. It was, in a word, a 'dream.'

Jackson pulled her carefully onto his lap, wrapping his arms around her as she cradled the ring in her palm. "Baby, if it's too soon, that's fine. I know I wasted a lot of time, but I don't want to waste any more."

"Jack-"

"So if you need more time, some time to think, or-"

"Jack."

She looked up and saw the deep lines around his mouth, the corners of his eyes, and between his brows.

"You're so stressed."

"I don't want to mess this up." He cleared his throat. "You really only get one shot at this if you do it right and if you do it wrong-"

"Jack!"

"Yeah?" He looked down at her and she could see how hard he was working to breath in and out.

"There's only one way you could mess this up."

"Really?" He swallowed hard enough that she could hear it. "How would I do that?"

"You haven't asked me yet."

His eyes opened wider and he looked at her, a little more confused than anything else. "I'm sorry, what?"

Laughing along with most of the group around them,

Hi`ilani shook her head. "You gave me a ring, but you haven't asked me the question."

"Well if we're doing the dwarf thing," grumbled Baron, "he gets to be Dopey."

Truck put a restraining hand on Train's shoulder. "I'll toss him over the fence, just say the word."

Mary grabbed at Truck's arm. "Shhh…"

Hi`ilani laughed and picked up Jackson's hand from her leg. She set the ring in his hand and gave him a gentle smile. "Ask me."

He picked up the ring between two fingers and held it gently as he cradled her face between his hands. "Will you marry-"

She kissed him, her hands falling to his shoulders pulling him close, slanting her lips over his. When she ran out of air she sat back and sighed at the dazed look in his eyes. "Yes, Jack. I'll marry you."

Train let out a shout, shocking them both.

When the others looked at him, he laughed out loud. "When the rest of the team comes back, they're going to be so mad they this missed all of this." He gave Jackson a satisfied smile. "But I got it on video."

Jackson let the others have a good laugh. He was busy sliding the ring on her finger.

GLOSSARY

Hawaiian Word Pronunciation Guide
Twelve Letters in the Hawaiian Alphabet: 5 vowels (a, e, i, o, u) and 7 consonants (h, k, l, m, n, p, w)

Pronouncing the Vowels
A = AH
E = EH
I = EE
O = OH
U = OO

And because the Hawaiian language was purely verbal until the arrival of the Missionaries in Hawaii, no letter is ever silent. It is a purely phonetical language.

The words that I'm entering into this glossary will also appear on my website/blog and will include pictures to help illustrate some of the words

Hawaiian Words in the Book: (in order of appearance)

Hiʻilani – name meaning 'beautiful heaven'

Ahfong – a surname of Chinese/Hawaiian descent

lauʻae – a flat leafed plant with a heady, clean scent

Kukui – a native plant called the candlenut tree. The tree is the state tree of Hawaii and can be distinguished by its silver-green leaves

Hale Koa Hotel – a hotel in Waikiki on the Island of Oʻahu – you must be a member of the military or a military dependent to stay at the hotel.

Kuli kuli e – phrase usually used for children, or those acting like them, asking them to 'be quiet'!

Mahalo – Thank you

muʻumuʻu – local garment developed from the neck to toe clothing of the missionary women

Aʻole pilikia – used after "Mahalo" when you want to say 'no worries' or 'no problem'

Ono – delicious

Kaleo – name meaning 'voice' or 'the voice'

Haole – foreigner the derogatory nature of the word can be negated by tone if you're in a group that understands the use

Kuʻu Home O Kahaluʻu – (song title) My dearest home in Kahaluʻu

Aloha ahiahi – Good Evening – Good Night

Tutu – Grandmother

kamaʻaina – local person, either born in Hawaii or has lived so long in the island they are like the people born there

Ewa side – the Western side of the Island

Pikake – plant and flower – tiny white jasmine on a climbing vine with dark green leaves

Kailani – name meaning beautiful water

Leilani – name meaning beautiful lei (garland of flowers)

Ukulele – small stringed instrument (looks like a guitar) based off of the design of a Portuguese instrument – developed in the 1800s

Moemoe – sleep – time to sleep

Honi – Hawaiian 'kiss' – a press of noses where the two breath in each other's exhaled breath – like mingling breath/souls

Haku lei – a flower garland made by winding or braiding the various items of flora together – one of the more time-consuming lei to make

Pidgin English Words and Phrases in the Book: (Pidigin is a mash up of a bunch of different languages that became a language of its own)

Auntie/Aunty – a woman close to you that's older by a generation – like family

K'den – okay then or all right – not overly enthusiastic

Calabash – like the large wooden/gourd bowl used to serve food – meaning 'like family'

karang his/your alas – guarded to make a local man wince – means to injure your family jewels

mo' bettah – better (literally 'more better)

Whatevah – whatever

Whatchu – what you

K – okay

Killah – killer

mu`u – short for mu`umu`u

Shaka – a friendly hand gesture made with the thumb and pinky finger extended and the three digits in the middle folded over in a loose fist

Boroboro – old and worn clothing, something to wear at home but not in front of company

Aiyah – a verbal expression of frustration like 'oh no!' Very common among asians

Buggah – describing a person, typically a male

Dinnah - dinner

Nevah – never

Fo' – for

Paniolo – a Hawaiian cowboy – the tradition comes from the hiring of Spanish cowboys to teach the Hawaiians to run ranches and ride horses

Bus' me up – literally 'bust me up' – meaning beat me up/mess me up

No get – don't get

Wassup – what's up

Gon' – goin

Wen' – went

Hea – here

Aftah – after

Slippah – slipper

Almos' – almost

One noddah – another

No make A – don't been an ass – don't show your ass

Other words

theBus – Seriously, that's the actual name of our public transit bus

O-Triple-C – OCCC – Oahu Community Correctional Center

Raffia – a dried fiber that is commonly used to make haku lei, what we use to wind around the center of the lei, binding the flowers together

ABOUT THE AUTHOR

Love - Romance - Books
    Aren't they all the same thing?
    Oh, I sure hope so!

I've been reading romance books for what seems like forever. When I was a teen, the days that I wasn't in dance class after school I'd go to the mall to wait for my mom to finish work for the day and my haunt of choice... Waldenbooks. (I think I just showed my age there.)

Whether it was Scottish Lairds, Medieval Knights, Regency Gents, Rough and Tumble Cowboys, or handsome modern Heroes, I loved them all! There was always another hero and heroine to follow through page after page of breathless love!
    Please Visit My Website - www.reinatorres.com

BB bookbub.com/authors/reina-torres
a amazon.com/author/reinatorresromance

<u>Sylvan City Alphas Series</u>

The Tiger's Innocent Bride
The Fighter

<u>Three Rivers Express Series</u>

Always, Ransom
Always, Wyeth
Always, Ellis

<u>Orsino Security Series</u>

Her Unbearable Protector
His UnBearable Touch
Their Unbearable Destiny

<u>St. Raphael, CA Series</u>

Finding Home
Playing With Fire
Healing Hearts
Taking a Chance

<u>Shapeshifters of Arcadia</u>

Beneath the Surface

<u>Ellingsford, Montana Series</u>

Stay With Me
Her Gentle Heart
Hold Her Close

<u>Other</u>

Too Much Bear
Home to Roost
Justice for Sloane

There are many more books in this fan fiction world than listed here, for an up-to-date list go to www.AcesPress.com

You can also visit our Amazon page at:
http://www.amazon.com/author/operationalpha

Special Forces: Operation Alpha World
Denise Agnew: Dangerous to Hold
Shauna Allen: Awakening Aubrey
Shauna Allen: Defending Danielle
Shauna Allen: Rescuing Rebekah
Shauna Allen: Saving Scarlett
Shauna Allen: Saving Grace
Brynne Asher: Blackburn
Jennifer Becker: Hiding Catherine
Julia Bright: Saving Lorelei
Julia Bright: Rescuing Amy
Victoria Bright: Surviving Savage
Victoria Bright: Going Ghost
Victoria Bright: Jostling Joker
Cara Carnes: Protecting Mari
Kendra Mei Chailyn: Beast
Kendra Mei Chailyn: Barbie
Kendra Mei Chailyn : Pitbull
Melissa Kay Clarke: Rescuing Annabeth
Melissa Kay Clarke: Safeguarding Miley
Samantha A. Cole: Handling Haven
Samantha A. Cole: Cheating the Devil
Sue Coletta: Hacked
Melissa Combs: Gallant

KaLyn Cooper: Rescuing Melina
Liz Crowe: Marking Mariah
Jordan Dane: Redemption for Avery
Jordan Dane: Fiona's Salvation
Riley Edwards: Protecting Olivia
Riley Edwards: Redeeming Violet
Riley Edwards, Recovering Ivy
Nicole Flockton: Protecting Maria
Nicole Flockton: Guarding Erin
Nicole Flockton: Guarding Suzie
Nicole Flockton: Guarding Brielle
Casey Hagen: Shielding Nebraska
Casey Hagen: Shielding Harlow
Casey Hagen: Shielding Josie
Casey Hagen: Shielding Blair
Desiree Holt: Protecting Maddie
Kathy Ivan: Saving Sarah
Kathy Ivan: Saving Savannah
Kathy Ivan: Saving Stephanie
Jesse Jacobson: Protecting Honor
Jesse Jacobson: Fighting for Honor
Jesse Jacobson: Defending Honor
Jesse Jacobson: Summer Breeze
Silver James: Rescue Moon
Silver James: SEAL Moon
Silver James: Assassin's Moon
Silver James: Under the Assassin's Moon
Becca Jameson: Saving Sofia
Kate Kinsley: Protecting Ava
Heather Long: Securing Arizona
Heather Long: Guarding Gertrude

Jenika Snow: Protecting Lily
Jen Talty: Burning Desire
Jen Talty: Burning Kiss
Jen Talty: Burning Skies
Jen Talty: Burning Lies
Jen Talty: Burning Heart
Megan Vernon: Protecting Us
Megan Vernon: Protecting Earth

Fire and Police: Operation Alpha World

Freya Barker: Burning for Autumn
KaLyn Cooper: Justice for Gwen
Aspen Drake: Sheltering Emma
Barb Han: Kace
Reina Torres: Justice for Sloane
Stacey Wilk: Stage Fright

As you know, this book included at least one character from Susan Stoker's books. To check out more, see below.

SEAL of Protection: Legacy Series

Securing Caite
Securing Brenae (novella) (April 2019)
Securing Sidney (May 2019)
Securing Piper (Sept 2019)
Securing Zoey (TBA)
Securing Avery (TBA)
Securing Kalee (TBA)

Delta Force Heroes Series

Rescuing Rayne (FREE!)
Rescuing Aimee (novella)
Rescuing Emily
Rescuing Harley
Marrying Emily
Rescuing Kassie
Rescuing Bryn
Rescuing Casey
Rescuing Sadie
Rescuing Wendy
Rescuing Mary
Rescuing Macie (April 2019)

Badge of Honor: Texas Heroes Series

Justice for Mackenzie (FREE!)
Justice for Mickie
Justice for Corrie

Justice for Laine (novella)
Shelter for Elizabeth
Justice for Boone
Shelter for Adeline
Shelter for Sophie
Justice for Erin
Justice for Milena
Shelter for Blythe
Justice for Hope
Shelter for Quinn
Shelter for Koren (July 2019)
Shelter for Penelope (Oct 2019)

SEAL of Protection Series

Protecting Caroline (FREE!)
Protecting Alabama
Protecting Fiona
Marrying Caroline (novella)
Protecting Summer
Protecting Cheyenne
Protecting Jessyka
Protecting Julie (novella)
Protecting Melody
Protecting the Future
Protecting Kiera (novella)
Protecting Alabama's Kids (novella)
Protecting Dakota

New York Times, USA Today and *Wall Street Journal*
Bestselling Author Susan Stoker has a heart as big as the
state of Tennessee where she lives, but this all American

girl has also spent the last fourteen years living in Missouri, California, Colorado, Indiana, and Texas. She's married to a retired Army man who now gets to follow *her* around the country.

She debuted her first series in 2014 and quickly followed that up with the SEAL of Protection Series, which solidified her love of writing and creating stories readers can get lost in.

If you enjoyed this book, or any book, please consider leaving a review. It's appreciated by authors more than you'll know.

www.stokeraces.com

www.AcesPress.com

susan@stokeraces.com

Made in United States
Cleveland, OH
18 November 2025

26239973R10134